Rave Reviews for Yesterday Mourning

"Yesterday Mourning is an inspirational, honest, and raw story that wraps itself around you as you delve into the complex and complicated dynamic of Yvette and Vera's family. Through the drama and emotional turmoil of their pasts, their struggle to reconcile and move forward in their lives is breathtaking as they are taught life lessons about loss, love, forgiveness, healing, and redemption. I don't think that anyone will come away from this story without feeling some emotional connection. Yesterday Mourning is an amazing story with a thoughtful and soul-searching message that will stay with you long after the last words have been read."

"This is a great book! If you love fiction and great writing, Yesterday Mourning is sure to satiate your literary curiosity! From the very beginning, Bryant draws you in with powerful imagery and rhythmic dialogue that makes the reader feel as though they are in the time and setting of the book. The characters are very relatable and the story told is one that all can empathize with, even if they haven't gone through similar situations themselves. For her first book, Bryant impressed and that speaks volumes to her dedication to her craft as a writer."

"Ms. Bryant's brilliantly descriptive style of storytelling is reminiscent of Baldwin's early years. Couple that with an intense, sometimes tear-jerking story told at a perfect pace and you've got a literary gem here worth reading again and again. Yesterday Mourning takes us on a worthwhile journey through the joys and pains of the human experience through a tale of every kind of love, hope, regret, and forgiveness."

"The author breathed life into each character with such true emotion. I felt as if I knew each character personally and I couldn't stop reading until I had finished the book. I am so looking forward to this author's next work. Well done!"

YESTERDAY MOURNING

A NOVEL

RENITA BRYANT

Yesterday Mourning (10th Anniversary Edition)

Copyright © 2013 and 2024 by Renita Bryant.

All rights reserved. No part of this book may be reproduced in any written, electronic, recording, or photocopying without written permission of the publisher or author.

This is a work of fiction. Names, characters, places, and incidents either are the product of the author's imagination or are used fictitiously. Any resemblance to actual persons, living or dead, events, or locales is entirely coincidental.

Books may be purchased in quantity and/or special sales by contacting the publisher.

MYND MATTERS IS A REGISTERED TRADEMARK

Mynd Matters Publishing
2690 Cobb Pkwy SE, Suite A5-375
Smyrna, GA 30080
www.myndmatterspublishing.com

978-1-963874-19-8 (pbk)
978-1-963874-20-4 (hdcv)
978-1-963874-21-1 (ebk)

SECOND EDITION

*For my mother,
the woman who taught me the value of words.
Keeping your memory & legacy alive will always
be my priority.*

Rest in peace and unconditional love.

PROLOGUE

I didn't know what to say. Two years had passed since I last laid eyes on him, and I had no clue what would be the first or final words spoken. Maybe I'd ask for an in-depth explanation as to why he didn't try harder to salvage the relationship we built—the love we shared.

While I wanted to hear his answers, my heart recognized that simple words wouldn't make our truth any less real. Our perspectives had changed because our lives had changed. Our interactions had transformed into something entirely different than the possibilities we would have imagined a few years ago.

A part of me wanted to run away in hopes of avoiding both him and the complexity of this moment—a moment built on the promise of closure. However, running away stopped being an option a long time ago, and as such, I got the privilege of sitting on a concrete step under an August Georgia sun waiting for my father to turn the corner into our cul-de-sac. I got to wonder whether he would try to hug me or engage in small talk—or do the unexpected and admit fault for the current state of our situation.

I wish things had been different. I wish he had made a different choice—one that involved me, or at least considered me. I replayed our conversations often, wondering whether I was too sensitive or whether he really was as heartless and selfish as I perceived him to be.

We were both mourning a loss—a wife, a mother. He yearned to feel her touch just as I longed to see her smile. Her voice had coached us both through the funeral, the holidays, and the random moments such as being in the grocery store and seeing a grapefruit and remembering how much she loved them. Both of us had changed hospital bed sheets, paged nurses, and authorized procedures while feeling her slip away from our hopeful grasps. The sting of tears on wishful cheeks was no less painful for either of us. Our tears just fell in two different states and for two very different reasons. The reasons were what hindered me from knowing what I should say to him.

I wished Zoe were here in my place. My sister was better with this sort of thing. Known for her honest and blatant approach, she'd stopped speaking to our father months before I discontinued conversation with him. For some reason, I felt the need to engage in pleasantries, hoping it would mask my hurt and disappointment. When it didn't, I knew the relationship was over. Zoe was entirely different. She lived by the "fool me once shame on you" philosophy, so he was ejected from her life long before he could brace himself for the impact.

Zoe and I lost our forty-two-year-old mother to a rare cancer that quickly advanced within three months. While that loss was painful, unexpected, and misunderstood, losing our father was even harder—harder because it happened through an unexplained chain of events that he authored. Harder because we still walked the same earth and breathed the same air, yet we'd found a way to disregard one another's presence. Harder because the one thing promised after our mother's death was that he would always be there for us—yet when he had the chance to prove it, he chose a different path.

A popular tune played through my cell, interrupting my thoughts. I looked down to see Zoe's name flashing across the screen. "Is he there yet?" Zoe didn't beat around the proverbial bush. She asked the question with a recognizable layer of resentment and disdain enveloping it.

"No, not yet. I'm sitting on the steps waiting." I looked up at a beautifully blue, cloudless sky and wondered why I couldn't get this type of natural perfection in Philadelphia. There, the sky was always either enclosed by clouds or had a dark grayish color that adumbrated torrential rain and canceled picnics. Don't mistake me. I love the culture and essence of Philly. I just wonder if it would take paying more in taxes to get a glimpse of sun every now and then.

"Why are you on the steps? It has to be about 100 degrees today. Are you trying to pass out?" Zoe's question brought me back to reality and diverted my attention to the tension that was waging war inside my body.

"I don't have a key, remember? Besides, I have a bottle of water, so I shouldn't get dehydrated." Zoe accepted my simple and somewhat true response. I didn't tell her that sitting on the steps reminds me of our childhood. I feel youthful and carefree—like every bad thing that had happened was a figment of my imagination. I wanted us to still play Red Light/Green Light or Mother, May I in the front yard. I smiled at thoughts of family barbecues and Christmas parties that were hosted here. The last time everyone had been at this address was right after the funeral. The uneasiness returned.

"Yvette, you're twenty-six and able to make your own decisions but I think you should wait in your rental car." Zoe wasn't letting this go.

"Why should I wait in the car? I can handle a little sun. It was this hot in Philly before I left." I thought about getting in the car to appease her but decided against it.

"You've been living up north for so long I don't think

you can handle this type of heat anymore." I laughed at Zoe's comment. As if the sun was a different one in Georgia than in Pennsylvania.

"Little sis, thanks for the concern. I'm sure I'll be okay." Zoe continued joking about my transition from southern belle to northerner, but I'd stopped listening. I could see a car with a man behind the wheel slowly turning onto the street.

"Hey, I think he's here," I said in a whisper. I don't know why I whispered, considering no one else could hear our conversation, especially the person in the dark green Jaguar pulling into the driveway.

"Does he look different? Is his car ridiculously obnoxious? Did he bring them?" I froze at the last question. "Them" was his new wife, Mary, and stepdaughter, Vera, although new may not be the proper term considering they were married about seven months after my mother died. That was one of the primary reasons for my lack of interest in meeting with him now. Zoe and I expected him to move forward and possibly remarry. We just never anticipated it being so quick and quiet. On more than one occasion, he suggested he was forced into marriage because of his position in the clergy and the potential rumors if he'd simply engaged in dating. Truth be told, my disapproval had more to do with how he elected to act versus what he needed to react to. His decisions had a direct impact on our lives that he never considered. I wish I knew more about his stepdaughter, though. Here he was electing to raise someone else's child but disregarding the two that housed his genes.

"No, I think he's alone." I cautiously stood while listening to his car shift from drive to park and then become eerily silent as the engine was turned off.

"Hey, let me call you back." I mouthed the words to Zoe,

but when I heard her say "What," I repeated it with the addition of sound.

"Okay, but call me as soon as he leaves, and don't let him get to you. You don't owe him anything, not even the acknowledgment of his presence."

A door opened and closed.

"He's there to give you the keys and get the rest of his crap…"

I heard footsteps on the paved cement.

"Anything else should've been managed through his expensive yet incompetent attorney. Yvette don't let him rattle you. He's not worth it." With that, Zoe and I said goodbye, and I turned to see my father standing at the bottom of the steps.

"Hello, Yvette." His greeting was hard to read—maybe because it was short and exact, no room for confusion.

I nodded a hello because my voice chose that very moment to betray me. I guess it agreed with Zoe. My father looked the same minus about fifteen pounds. He was an average 5'9" with broad shoulders, a low fade haircut, and a dark complexion. He had a pair of fake reading glasses sitting atop his nose in an attempt to convince the world that his education wasn't obtained on neighborhood street corners but instead in immaculately dressed buildings with Corinthian columns and Latin inscriptions over large oak doorways. I looked down to see his camel-colored Kenneth Coles pacing in one square as he folded and unfolded his hands. He needed a manicure—he always needed a manicure. I almost smiled to myself when considering the small sign that spoke volumes to a past his future had never been able to escape. I stared at the argyle sweater vest, khaki shorts, and green short-sleeved polo, as if seeing the colors for the first time. My eyes slowly surveyed the luxury car sitting in the driveway, his shined designer shoes tapping on the concrete, and the thin spectacles on the end of his nose. I wondered how much of my mother's insurance money had been used to create his new image, his new life.

During one of our final conversations (arguments), he spoke a truth that I'd been trying to avoid. " This is business." Those simple words stung my ears and simultaneously turned the part of my heart that had once loved and adored him to stone. We had become those people, that family. Our thoughts and decisions were now shared through attorneys and our accomplishments and life events through social media. When we did engage in conversation, which is how I came to hear those three words, it was as two professionals trying to resolve differing interests in a part of the estate—the house.

When my mother died, we learned the house was solely in her name. She didn't have a will and therefore, interest in the property became equally split among her beneficiaries. Zoe wanted nothing to do with the house and after a few months, my father felt the same way. They both wanted to sell while I saw a need to keep it in the family. Conversations grew tense, relationships suffered, and in the end, my father forced us to buy him out of his share. It was one thing to disagree on how to manage the house. It was another to make your grieving daughters write you a check.

I moved to the side as he ascended all four steps to the front door. I caught a glimpse of myself in one of the front windows. From my caramel-colored skin to my high cheekbones and full lips, I was the perfect blend of my parents. My eyes were deeply set like my mother's but with the intensity of my father's. I was an independent thinker like my mother but spoke with a pastor's passion, which came from my father. I had wide hips and an ample bosom like both sides of my family. I was their child, a product of their union. I frowned at the image.

Stepping through the doorway was akin to taking a trip back in time. Nothing had really changed, and I couldn't decide if I was happy, sad, or indifferent. I looked around the living room, allowing my eyes to rest on every detail—pictures, trophies, paintings, and figurines. I became lightheaded as my mind discerned the fullness of the moment. It'd been over a year since the estate administrator, my father, had allowed me access to this space. Finally, after all the petty comments, endless arguments, and needless conversations, I was standing in the home that raised me, shielded me, and cradled me. My first experience mopping floors, washing dishes, and making beds had been here. I shared first kisses with boyfriends on the smoke gray leather loveseat and cried tears over breakups across the canopy bed in my old room. This house was like a member of the family, another entity in our relationship. It was more than stepping back into a building, I was returning to my mother's arms. We were a family, a complete unit, when we lived here. That's precisely when the sadness washed over me. This house, this space, represented everything I once had. I no longer had a mother, or even a father it seemed; my sister was in college creating her own memories, and my address now existed above the Mason-Dixon. Seconds ago, I was able to feel the love of this place, but now, now I just felt like a waif who yearns for times that will never return.

I wiped away the tears that threatened to fall and moved deeper into the room. My eyes continued to alight on so many small things that showed the touch of my mother. This was her vision, her future. It felt wrong to feel sadness when being in this space had been such a materialization of success for her. Eighteen years old and a recent high school graduate, she considered having me a blessing. I felt indebted for such a significant show of love. I always wondered if I would've made the same choice given her circumstances. Her life was a testament to the power of endurance and strength. It showed achievement is only limited by one's perseverance. Although she began as a secretary for the Department of Defense, she worked hard and later became one of the highest-ranking civilian managers within the Office of Budget and Finance. When my seventh-grade teacher had the class write stories about our respective heroes, my mother quickly came to mind. She'd always been exceptional in my eyes.

My mood shifted, the negativity eased, and I felt joy—happiness even. She was my real-life hero. Those words repeated in my head. At one point in the past my father had held the same title. His love had been just as strong and his determination just as noble. I wanted to connect with that life again. But while our past was meaningful, my heart still felt pangs of resentment for how he'd handled the most recent events. This house had been important to our family and he of all people should've fought harder to keep it.

As much as I wanted to be alone and exclude him from the history and love preserved in this space, I also wanted to share it with someone. Someone that would understand the inside jokes like a stain on the carpet or a surface scratch on the wall. Someone that had the privilege of sharing a smile with my mother while standing at the his-and-hers sink in the morning as they both prepared for work. Someone whose embrace had always made me feel safe and cherished. That someone was currently packing his final items and most likely experiencing similar feelings of déjà vu. It was time to build bridges and overcome the odds.

I walked toward the bedroom, trying to think of ways to start a conversation. Maybe I could make a joke or lead with a "remember when" moment. I felt anxious but couldn't determine why. In the past, this house represented more than documents and estate filings. It was our home, and I wanted him to know how much that mattered. I needed us to put the past where it belonged and possibly be a family again. I proceeded with my mental pacing until I felt comfortable enough to actually open my mouth. Before I could speak, he exited the master bedroom with a small box filled to the brim. I could see the wheels turning in his head, wondering if he'd forgot something, and then, as if on cue, he shrugged his shoulders and continued walking. He looked up at me, smiled, and continued toward the front door. I felt a pang of anger as I watched his carefree stride and dismissal of our history. Each step sounded so final. It was all a bit too surreal. I wanted to speak, to say something that would be equally hurtful. I wanted to assault his heart in the same manner that his designer shoes were attacking my mother's hardwood floor. Suddenly he turned around, and the echoes stopped bouncing off the walls.

"I left the keys on the kitchen counter. Silver is for the main door, and gold is for the garage door. If you're keeping the alarm, call the company on Monday and have them re-activate the account in your name." He said all of this like a stranger that had never stood at that sink or shared any inside jokes. My thoughts were plagued with the image of him shrugging away the memories of this house, of our past, and moving forward with ease and disinterest. Later, I would consider how much of an impact that small action had on how I perceived our fateful day.

I slowly walked out of the door and back into the Georgia sun. The anxiety I'd felt moments before had given way to resignation. I looked at him from the top of the steps, knowing that the next time we saw one another would be at a table covered with legal documents and seats filled by attorneys and agents. This was our last private father-daughter moment. I'd get married, and he wouldn't walk me down the aisle. I'd have children that would never know the touch of his hand or the span of his smile. He would fill pews in towns across Georgia, and my ears would never bear witness to his message. He was now someone else's father, and I was simply a memory bottled within his past. We were two people whose once melodic and soulful rhythm had become wildly staccato. We only knew the history of one another, and because of everything that had happened, our future selves could not exist in a shared world. We were strangers that just so happened to have shared a past. By twenty-six, I'd suffered the loss of two parents, one to terminal disease and the other to life's complications.

He looked over at me, and I sensed hesitation before he finally entered his car and started the engine. Within seconds, he was turning onto the main road with only taillights as a sign he'd ever been here. Sometimes I think about what could've been. I almost shed a tear for the father I will never know and the memories we'll never share.

I never did figure out what to say to him or how to say it. Instead, I took the words that have been etched on my heart and in my brain and filed them under emotional resignation. I used those thoughts to remind me of the life I left behind, of a love that failed to exist above conditions.

CHAPTER 1

YVETTE

That was sixteen years ago. Lately, I've thought about our fateful day more often than not. Maybe it's because Kayla, my twelve-year-old daughter, found a few photographs and started asking questions about people who helped define her genetic makeup. Or it could be because I'm packing a suitcase for a weeklong trip to Georgia, where my head will rest under the roof where final goodbyes were never expressed, goodbyes that still seem confined within the walls and floorboards. Maybe it's because my forty-second birthday is in a few weeks, and I'm terrified of getting the same earth-shattering news that was delivered to my mother months after she crossed this bridge. In some ways, it's probably attributable to all three, which makes my anxiety even more pronounced and more than a little real.

Watching the rear taillights of his car turn the corner was so stabilizing for me. I always believed it stilled an urging in my spirit that used to require and request more from those who spoke of everlasting and unconditional love. But when the person that says they will be there to support you and sacrifice for you or simply love you the way you need to be loved doesn't—because he isn't capable of doing so—your understanding evolves into a feeling that transcends hatred and hurt. It somehow bypasses the emotions that accompany caring and instead migrates to not having any feeling at all. It settles into a level of indifference unmatched by any spite or unwavering ill will.

Some days I looked at Kayla and wondered if she would ever know this degree of emptiness. I tried to do everything in my power to mitigate that risk, but I realized I couldn't protect her from life. Trying to shield her from all of the bad things will presumably wind up placing her directly in harm's way. She must be exposed to some emotional upsets in order to handle the highs and lows of the journey. At least that's what I told myself so I didn't feel like a failed parent. Even now, I watch her as she watches me pack my toiletries, and I want to wrap her in my arms and never let go.

Understand that I love my child with everything in me. I'm certain my mother loved me with everything she had. But even as my heart registered the beauty of that truth, it also knew her love for me wasn't enough to protect me from her death. It wasn't enough to still the tears or hush the cries. Not until I gave birth could I fully comprehend how difficult it must be to leave this world before your child, how heavy the burden must be to look her in the eyes while knowing your life is nearing its end, to grasp the reality that you won't be able to provide any comfort because her very suffering is the effect of your causing. I couldn't fathom how intense the internal struggle of wanting to spend your last moments with the being that you birthed and nursed and reared while also wanting to push her away because the very notion of your death is hurting her. My mother had to watch me walk in and out of her hospital room every day. She was forced to come face to face with her own feelings of failure. A parent is supposed to always be there for her children. How could she feel fulfilled in her final moments, when she knew Zoe and I were about to plan her funeral? Internally, I always struggled through this revelation. I fought back tears when considering that our presence denied her the ability to find peace in the end.

About three years after sitting on those front steps, I stopped looking for answers and instead chose to move forward with the hand I was dealt. But after my gynecologist confirmed my pregnancy, the questions crept back in. While they started as fleeting thoughts, they evolved into well-designed scenes with in-depth dialogue. Now, with my October birthday in the near future, they are constant reminders that I'm mortal—mortal enough to leave this earth without so much as a goodbye to my family, my friends, or the divine miracle that I housed for nine months. I'm mortal enough to waste away in front of my daughter, leaving only distorted images of who I was and how I lived. My shoulders caved inward and I shed a tear for the knowledge that accepting my mortality meant accepting that one day I'd cause my child the greatest hurt a daughter could know. One day, I would leave her.

CHAPTER 2

VERA

"We'll be there in about twenty minutes, mom," I said hurriedly into the cell phone while struggling to balance it between my ear and right shoulder.

I'd checked the time occasionally over the past hour and was acutely aware of how far we were behind schedule. For some reason, every dress in my closet felt inappropriate or inadequate and I couldn't bring myself to spend the money on something new. I spotted a cap-sleeved, semi-formal gown and pulled it from the hanger. The sheer black top layer of the knee-length dress was accented with an eggshell-trimmed ruffle front that stopped short of the satin sash at the waist. I'd only worn the dress twice, once to a romantic dinner date with my husband Damien and another time a few months later when I attended a reception for the mayor. It would have to do.

Damien entered the bedroom as I slipped into the two-toned Mary Janes and grabbed a satin black clutch from the armoire.

"Vera, please don't be late. This is really important to your father, and to me." I wanted to roll my eyes at mom's guilt trip.

"I know, Mom. Damien just walked in, so let me finish getting ready, and we'll be there as soon as we can."

Damien caught the phone just as it slipped from my grasp.

"Good catch," I remarked as my husband's smiling eyes met mine.

"I'm an all-around athlete, baby," he replied jokingly.

I looked in the mirror and realized I must've gotten sidetracked at some point because I was wearing only one earring. I checked the dresser and on the bed underneath the hangers and rejected outfits but didn't find it.

"Sweetheart, have you seen my other earring?" I asked as Damien stepped out of the bathroom with my antique pearl and marcasite earring dangling from his right hand.

"You mean this?" He stepped backward into the bathroom as I reached for my missing accessory.

"Damien, we're already running late. Hand over the earring."

I tilted my head sideways and gave him a sweet but serious look. Instead of placing the earring in my outstretched hand, he turned me toward the mirror and proceeded to put it in my ear. His large hands gently grazed my cheek sending a slight flurry through my body.

Once finished, he stood behind me with his arms around my waist.

"May I just say that you look incredibly beautiful this evening," he whispered into my now adorned ear.

"Thank you for being you," I replied as I closed my eyes and allowed my body to relax and settle comfortably into his arms. Damien's lips felt soft against my neck, and I remembered why I fell for him all those years ago. He'd been far from perfect as a boyfriend but had matured into a great husband.

We'd met while both attending the University of Central Georgia. I was obtaining my bachelor's degree in Secondary Education, and he was a defensive end on the football team and occasionally attended classes. During my junior year, I worked as a staff writer on the Wildcat Weekly, the student newspaper. After an impressive homecoming game, I was given an assignment to interview Damien 'Pass Rush' Robinson. He'd been much bigger and more attractive in person, and I found myself at a loss for words. I'd stumbled through most of the interview even though I had copious notes since I didn't know much about the mechanics of football. He pretended not to notice but I could see how much he was enjoying my discomfort. After he answered a few questions about his preparation and motivation regarding the sport, he turned the tables and asked questions about me. Three hours later, we were talking and laughing like old friends and I'd forgotten all about the article. Ten years and a daughter later, we were happily married and running late to my parent's anniversary celebration.

"Mommy, Daddy, I can't find my other shoe."

I looked down to find our seven-year-old daughter, Annie, standing in the doorway with one shoe in hand.

"Did you check the shoebox?" I asked with both eyes still closed.

"Um, no. Wait, which box is it?"

I shifted to face Damien.

"Can you help find her shoe while I finish up in here? I'm pretty sure it's in the shoebox in her closet or under the bed."

"Of course, take your time. Well, not exactly, since we can't be late, but you get the idea," Damien said as he gave me a lingering smile and a pat on the hip.

I watched him through the mirror and couldn't help but feel an overwhelming sense of fortune. He was an attentive husband, a loving father, and quite pleasing to the eyes. His black semi-formal suit accentuated his broad shoulders and slightly bowed legs. I enjoyed watching him walk into and out of a room as if for the very first time. At night, we'd lie in bed talking about anything and everything, just like when we first met. I'd run my fingers along his chiseled jawline while staring at the specks of green in his brown eyes. They were always so caring and sincere. I felt fortunate to share a bed and a lifetime with that fine man.

A wave of heat came over me and I blinked to focus. I wasn't sure if it was thoughts of Damien or something else that caused my body's reaction. Three months ago we decided we were ready to have another baby. With Annie, we'd conceived a few weeks after I'd stopped taking birth control. This time, things weren't happening as quickly and Damien was growing worried. Although I hadn't taken a pregnancy test, I felt certain I was carrying our second child. Damien wanted me to take a test every week but after the first few weeks, I grew frustrated with the anxiety and disappointment. My body seemed to be working against me and I couldn't take the constant feelings of failure. Instead, we agreed to wait until after the anniversary celebration to find out.

I applied my makeup as quickly as humanly possible, grabbed a clutch, and exited the bedroom. I found Damien and Annie standing near the door that leads out to our garage.

"Mommy, we found my shoe!" Annie said excitedly.

"That's great missy, where was it?" I glanced at Damien as I hand-brushed Annie's ponytail.

"It was in the shoebox, duh!" Annie hit her hand to her forehead as she chuckled at her own response. Damien and I laughed at the humor of a seven-year-old and headed out the door.

Once settled in the car, I called my mother to let her know we were officially on the way. If traffic was light, we'd arrive at exactly seven o'clock. She wasn't pleased but at least we wouldn't be late.

The celebration was being hosted at the Manor House, an upscale country club on the outskirts of town. We'd attended a few functions there over the past few years, but tonight was special. Primarily because everyone present was there to honor the powerful and enduring love between my mother and stepfather. I'd always been amazed by how effortless it seemed. They communicated without words and when they did speak, it was with respect and adoration. I looked at Damien and silently prayed we'd continue to have a similar connection. Because my husband's parents had divorced when he was thirteen, he struggled to understand the notion of forever and unconditional love. His father had fallen into the cliché of having an affair with an office assistant while his mother pretended not to abuse anti-depressants. I wasn't one to judge his past, considering the tumultuous relationship between my mother and biological father. However, in the back of my mind, I wondered if our individual wounds would one day upend everything we were building.

The Pastor—an affectionate and accurate nickname I used for my stepfather—had been a perfectly-timed Godsend. While I wish he'd entered my life sooner, I was appreciative he'd been around at all. At first, I'd been distant due to my mother's curse for having subpar taste in men. She would bring home the most deplorable dates. I wasn't sure if she enjoyed the attention of a new boo or if her radar had simply been turned off and instead replaced with a 'Welcome All' sign. As a teenager, I grew accustomed to giving them the third degree while they smiled and tried to win my acceptance. I wasn't interested in a new father or a new life but regardless of my icy exterior and unpleasant nature, they rarely got the hint. My mother, on the other hand, chased the newness. She was focused on being a wife and living with her teen daughter in a two-bedroom apartment without a husband wasn't her ideal and wouldn't suffice. She had goals and a plan.

After my father left the picture, I assumed the bond between my mother and me would strengthen. I envisioned us traveling the world and enjoying life-changing adventures. Up to that point, my life had been confined to a small town and limited experiences, I yearned for more. I used books to escape for as long as I could, but eventually, I needed the fantasy to become my reality. I wanted us to take pictures of exotic animals while on safari at Kruger Park, stroll the Queen's Necklace in Mumbai while watching the sunset over the Arabian Sea, take in the Symphony of Lights from Tsim Sha Tsui in Hong Kong, and be amazed by the grandness of Aya Sofia and the Blue Mosque in Istanbul. In my mind, we would be inseparable, and no man would ever change that. In my mind, my biological father would eventually realize how special we were and plead for our forgiveness. We would both laugh at him while responding with a firm and final, *Nah*.

Then one day, something happened. She introduced me to someone new. A man that wasn't so deplorable and intolerable. Seeing them together felt more authentic, even pleasant. They fell into a natural cadence I'd not witnessed with the other men she'd once shared her time. As a result, I lowered my barriers a bit.

He was a pastor, which meant a new ritual of attending church every Sunday and Bible study every Wednesday. While not my favorite pastime, church was quite different from my mind's fabrications. I was intrigued by the characters and stories in the Bible and, within two months, volunteered to lead the children's Sunday School class. During that same time, my mother's relationship with the Pastor continued to blossom. I found myself alone many nights and feeling lonely even when she was home. It wasn't that our relationship was nonexistent, it just didn't feel fully realized. Maybe stunted is a better way to describe it. She did more for me than with me. She believed having a father figure in my life would somehow fill a gap in our lives, in our household. My eyes saw a gaping hole that wouldn't be filled simply because she'd brought home a man.

The Pastor was decent and made my mother happy. After the tumultuous relationship with my father, treating her with respect and decency was the minimum requirement. While his brokenness may have been different from my mother's, he was damaged, nonetheless. It was years before I was privy to the whole story, but in short, his wife had died and his daughters had abandoned him. Based on the whispered conversations I'd overheard, I was sure the decision was driven by his daughter Yvette's selfishness. If only she'd known…

The cell in my clutch vibrated twice. It was a text from my stepsister Zoe. I typed 'Next week? Okay, we're looking forward to it' in response to her question and muted the phone.

I couldn't believe what we were planning. After all these years, I doubted it'd make a difference. People don't just let go of anger and resentment so easily. Zoe was convinced we were doing the right thing, but I wasn't so sure. The entire plan would most likely blow up in our faces. If things didn't work out, I was the one with the most to lose.

A heaviness tried to descend upon my mood but I refused to let it get the best of me. Why should I feel guilty? I hadn't done anything wrong. For an instant, I was transported back in time to a sunny afternoon where that wasn't so much the case. I exhaled deeply then shook away images of crumbled envelopes and tried instead to focus on all the good things in my life, the things I'd done right. A couple of years after my parents exchanged vows, I started referring to the Pastor as my father. He had earned the title and we both knew it was time.

Damien squeezed my hand and asked if everything was okay. I could have told him every thought that was consuming my mind but when I looked at my husband, in that moment, everything was perfect.

CHAPTER 3

YVETTE

The B concourse at Philadelphia International Airport was always busy. My job caused me to become a frequent flyer, and fortunately, I was able to quickly check-in, breeze through security, and arrive at the gate with forty-five minutes to spare. I flipped through an Essence magazine, trying to find an article that could hold my attention for more than a few minutes. I don't know why I felt so anxious. I'd been to Georgia countless times over the past sixteen years. There were family reunions, graduations, weddings, and the occasional weekend getaway from the fast pace of Philadelphia.

There was an unexplained knot in my stomach, though. I felt it as I gave my boarding pass to the woman at the kiosk. I couldn't ignore it as I found my seat on the plane and put my carry-on bag into the overhead compartment. As the plane lifted into the air and I flew high above the city of brotherly love, something felt terribly wrong.

I shook my head as if trying to shake away the feelings altogether. It had been a few months since I was last on a plane heading south. Somehow, I forgot that this tenseness was nothing new. I always wondered if I would run into him at the local mall—which has never happened. For recreation, I'd think through detailed conversations of how our chance meeting would unfold. Years ago, I wanted to see him. I wanted us to bump into one another and then head over to a coffee shop for a chai latté and a few apologies. I needed him to explain so many things, but that never happened. The hope I once had for a chance encounter dissipated more with each passing year until, finally, no hope remained. It is amazing how one can yearn for something with such intensity while at the same time loathing it, or in my case, loathing the person who would help the dream materialize. I lost so many things sixteen years ago, and hope was one of the first on the list.

Three days before my mother died, her eyes told the story of her battle with hope. I remember the scene vividly. We were at the house, and she was lying in bed in the fetal position. Her body was frail from the combination of medications flowing through her veins and an inability to keep food down, resulting in massive weight loss. The hospice gown was loosely wrapped around her weakened body. While we tried to keep her looking and smelling as fresh as possible, she was starting to tire of constantly being changed and moved. On this particular day, I looked over and saw her trying to shift her body. Her gestures were subtle, almost nonexistent due to a lack of strength. Her body was competing against her mind, and it was upsetting her more and more.

Zoe and I had bought her one of those huge, triangle-shaped pillows that lift a person's head or feet by creating a gradual incline. I asked if she wanted me to help her up onto the pillow, and while her eyes pleaded yes, she mouthed, No. My mother had always been determined. She was not one to accept defeat easily or at all. Even though she gave birth to me four days after her eighteenth birthday, she went on to finish high school and undergrad and become the first person in our family to get a master's degree. She graduated with honors and was the smartest person I'd ever known. No, she didn't accept defeat easily. Therefore, watching her struggle for something as simple as an inch was especially difficult.

I watched as she tried to move herself and readjust, but she again lost the battle. Finally, she whispered, "Help me." I quickly went to her aid, putting her arms around my neck and holding the back of her head in my left hand while using my right hand to support her. I told her I was going to slowly lift her up to the pillow. I felt a slight squeeze on my arm and looked at her. She mouthed, "Wait," which meant she was afraid. She was in so much pain that the thought of more was unbearable.

I smiled down at her and told her not to worry. I said with every bit of strength in me, "Mommy, just hold on to me, and I'll make sure you're comfortable. I promise not to let anything happen to you."

She clasped her hands behind my head, and I lifted her upper body as carefully and gently as I knew how. When I placed her down, I said, "See, I told you I wouldn't let anything happen to you."

I started to pull away, but I felt her tighten her grip around my back. She held me to her and gave me all of the love left in her body. She held me so tightly that I was initially surprised and then saddened. I knew it wasn't a regular hug. She whispered she loved me, and I whispered the same. I heard the words only a hug like that could replace. She was telling me all the things I needed to hear, not just for the present but for the future I would have to live without her. That moment said things life wouldn't allow her to say, like how beautiful I looked in my wedding gown and how proud she was of everything I'd accomplished. Our embrace equaled encouragement through the birth of one child and the strength to overcome the loss of another. She told me I could do and be all things if I refused to be paralyzed by fear. I held onto her with more vigor and reliance. In that moment, we were one being. We became one honesty, one truth. A few seconds later, she released her grip and turned her head to the side as tears stained her cheeks. My mother had just transferred a lifetime of hope from her body into mine. I believe she knew what was about to happen, not only a few days later but years into the future. She knew I'd find myself feeling alone and void of so many things, so she tried to give me the little she had left. It was her last, yet most selfless, act as my parent.

Not until I reached my thirties did I realize how young my mother had been when she left this world. When I was a teen or even in my early twenties, people in their forties seemed ancient and disconnected from my modern world. But when I looked up and saw the limits of a life lived, the unfulfilled dreams and aspirations of a young forty-two-year-old woman, my mother, I mourned even more. It was always easy to recognize the things in my life I'd be forced to experience without her. But not until I reached those years did I consider the life she wouldn't get to live.

I turned my head toward the window and looked out at the cumulus clouds filling the sky. Miles below, day was turning into night. But here, above the clouds, everything was peaceful and constant. The uneasiness dissipated, and things looked so clear.

৯ ৶

I woke up as the plane's wheels touched down. I didn't remember dozing off, but I was a little upset that I'd missed the snack cart. My mouth was dry, and I was counting on some roasted peanuts and a ginger ale to hold me over until dinner. The pilot instructed everyone to remain seated until we were safely parked at the gate. Cell phones started vibrating and ringing as they were powered on. The quiet rumbling grew as people called their loved ones to announce their official arrival. I turned on my cell and checked my voicemail. There was a call from my husband and daughter reminding me that they loved me and wished me a safe flight. I smiled at the sound of their voices. There was a call from Zoe confirming she was at the airport and would meet me directly outside of the baggage claim. I almost laughed out loud at this message because Hartsfield International Airport has about ten exit doors, and she said everything except which one. I had one additional message from my father's oldest sister asking me to call her when I got to town. I returned my husband's call first, and my daughter answered on the second ring.

"Hiiii, Mom," Kayla said in a singsong voice.

"Hello, my love." I smiled again, thinking about her adorable little face and how much I already missed her.

"How was your flight? Are you with Auntie Zoe yet?" she innocently inquired.

"The flight was nice because I slept through most of it. I'll be with your aunt in a few minutes. I haven't gotten to baggage claim just yet."

Kayla adored Zoe, and every few months or so, I considered moving back to Georgia so she could spend more time with her extended family. When Kayla turned two, Christopher and I contemplated having more children and decided we were pleased with giving all of our love and support to our daughter. Over the years, I started to dream about having another baby—a son. I loved my husband and saw how great he was as a father, and believed having a son would complete our family. The concept of "completing" was ironic, though, because we were already a complete family. Christopher wanted to know if I was searching for more meaning in my life and if I thought a child would provide some contentment. Although I would never admit it to him, he was probably right. There was an increased feeling of emptiness and discontent during my waking hours. As Kayla started to grow and depend on me for less, I panicked. How would I define my life and my purpose if not for the dependence of my child?

In the end, it wasn't meant to be. We had one miscarriage, and I knew neither of us wanted to face that degree of uncertainty and anguish ever again. Luckily, we drew closer during the months that followed, and our marriage remained stable and strong. Even though we couldn't give Kayla a sibling, someone with whom she could develop a closeness and familiarity, we gave her everything we had, unselfishly and unashamedly.

"Yvette, are you there?" I chuckled and told my husband that I was indeed still on the line. We discussed the flight and a few news headlines as I deplaned, walked to the train, and took the final escalator up to the baggage claim. Even after years of marriage, I enjoyed the sound of Christopher's voice. It's so calming and peaceful. He's not a harsh, loud man. He was very deliberate and thoughtful, as evidenced by the first time I heard him speak.

We met one Saturday afternoon at a coffee shop in the Manayunk neighborhood of Philadelphia. I was there for a book club meeting, and he was there working on his dissertation. We debate the actual events of that day because I believe he was too engrossed in his paper to notice me, and he says he was trying not to show just how interested and eager he felt. One thing on which we both agree is the touch. Christopher walked up to the register to order his second cup of coffee just as I turned to walk away with my tea. An electric shock ran through me as I lightly brushed past him. I turned to apologize, but no words came out. He looked at me with a knowing smile, and at that moment, we felt connected. We both politely laughed and went back to doing the things that had brought us to our meeting place.

At two o'clock, my meeting ended, and I turned to leave. I no longer saw the stranger sitting in the corner staring at his laptop while surrounded by books. Something inside of me frowned. As I crossed the street and headed toward my car, I heard footsteps and a faint, "Excuse me." I hesitantly turned and found the coffee shop stranger jogging toward me. I smiled up at him as he extended his hand and simply said, "I've been waiting for you."

That chance meeting was six months prior to my date with those front steps under an August Georgia sun. I remember flying back to Philadelphia feeling emotionally drained and confused. Christopher helped me sort through my feelings and get back to the level of focus that I had when we first met. He was encouraging, supportive, and respectful of my vulnerability. I always knew he was the only person that could have stood beside me during that time in my life. I'd dated several guys over the course of my journey, but Christopher was different. His natural inclination had always been to protect, provide, and pour into me. I tried to shut him out several times, and regardless of my outbursts or threats to leave him, he didn't hold a grudge. He simply held me tighter and became more devoted in his love for me. Looking back, he had plenty of reasons and opportunities to walk away. His decision to remain is what continues to fuel our mutual commitment.

"Christopher, I just spotted Zoe."

My sister was standing among a massive crowd of people waiting to greet their respective friends and family. My smile broadened as we locked eyes.

"Yvette!" Zoe ran over, and we embraced tightly and knowingly. Christopher asked me to give Zoe and the family his best as we exchanged goodbyes and I love yous. He then put Kayla on the line so she could speak to her favorite aunt. I handed my cell to Zoe and watched her face light up yet again.

"Is this my favorite niece?" Zoe laughed at Kayla's response as we walked toward the exit doors. Zoe promised to take care of me and fly up to Philadelphia to visit before the year ended. She didn't stop making promises until we were lifting my bag into the trunk of her Volkswagen and exiting the airport.

CHAPTER 4

YVETTE

The car ride produced feelings of nostalgia. Seeing the green grass and trees alongside Interstate 75 reminded me of the weekend drives to Lenox Mall and family vacations to Six Flags.

I smiled at memories of unplanned road trips to Atlanta from Tallahassee with college classmates and old boyfriends. Soon after I moved to Philadelphia, this drive became the link to my family, my refuge. It was the one thing standing between the airport and the house. Back then, I fought it at every turn and every exit. It was merely something holding me back from where I wanted to be. Right now, it felt like a journey that I needed to experience. Each exit represented a memory. Memories that shaped me and helped frame the way I see the world. Even though this was how I felt, in my head, it sounded too "deep." It was far too sentimental for a casual car ride.

I smiled to myself and continued telling Zoe about Kayla's latest shenanigans. We laughed at her innocence and boldness, knowing that because she gets both of those from me, I couldn't be upset.

"She doesn't just tell us she wants a puppy. No, not my child. She decides to give us a full presentation on the benefits of having a puppy, including, and I quote, increasing her sense of responsibility and bringing positive energy into the house."

"My niece is too much," Zoe said between laughs.

"Yeah, she is. Know that when I say a presentation, I mean it. She had note cards with bullet points on them. She even gave a demonstration on how she would clean up after Lucky—oh, yeah, because she's already named the dog. Although Christopher and I were already debating whether or not we're going to surprise her with a dog for Christmas, I appreciated her effort."

"Admit it, Kayla got it honestly. Didn't you do the same thing to mom and dad?"

I brought my hand to my forehead, almost regretting how honestly Kayla got it. The summer between sophomore and junior year in high school was all about getting a car. We lived in a small town and it felt as though everyone else in my class was shopping for a car and I didn't want to be the only one without one. I knew asking my parents directly would result in a fast and resolute no. Instead, I used creativity and made my appeal in a less typical way. I wrote a short play with the overall message being that parents can prove how much they love and trust their children by giving them responsibility beyond chore but with things like cars. I had a few friends and cousins play minor roles in the production, and I provided light snacks for my parents to enjoy as they watched. Even though they seemed impressed by my thoroughness, I didn't get a car that summer. But the next year, my dad drove his pickup truck and let me drive his Nissan Pathfinder until I graduated.

I looked over at my sister, whose hand was clasped over her mouth to stifle back thunderous laughter, and I suddenly felt a wave of sadness. Being in the same space with her always exposed my vulnerability. It reminded me of the past, a time when we both existed in innocence and felt protected from the world. A time when there was nothing called grief, and depression was merely a word grownups threw around when they were having a bad day. We became life vests for one another, and that reality has kept our relationship in a place of completeness that many don't comprehend. It's evident in the way we communicate and resolve problems. Zoe and I can't fight because we recognize the shortness and unpredictability of life. One argument could equal a lifetime of regret. I reached over and took her hand. She looked at me, and without a word, she understood.

I don't remember our conversation or feeling sad for the rest of the drive. Zoe found an ingenious way to switch the path that I was heading down by finding a superficial topic that evoked mirrored emotion. Fortunately, we were still on the topic when we pulled into the subdivision and parked in the garage.

The house was different than I remembered. Zoe had painted the shutters, planted a few more trees, and installed a pool in the backyard. Even with all of her effort, the changes on the outside couldn't diminish the presence of a past on the inside. While she'd redesigned the kitchen, installed new carpeting, painted the walls, and hung beautiful artwork, I knew the space, and it knew me. There was a familiarity I always tried to avoid but never quite could.

I'd been to the house since that fateful day. A few years after she graduated, I helped Zoe move in. When Christopher and Kayla would come with me to Georgia, we got a hotel room, which Christopher thought was wasteful since Zoe and I both have equal ownership of the house. For me, it was about not being a burden to my sister. On solo trips, however, I always slept at Zoe's. It was home regardless of where my mail was being delivered.

I went to the guest bedroom and set my suitcase beside the bed. I couldn't put my finger on it but something about the house felt unsettled. I moved everything from the bag to either the closet or dresser. I continued until most of my clothes were hanging, my shoes were lining the closet floor, and my toiletries were in a neat row on the dresser. I didn't notice the changes in the room until I finally collapsed onto the bed. On the nightstands, Zoe had added more pictures of Mom. I smiled while running my fingers across the frames. She was beautiful both inside and out, and it felt good to see her smile again—no signs of pain, of cancer, of hopelessness.

My freshman year of college, my parents surprised me with a car. Tucked under one of the windshield wipers was the script from my play. I was so overwhelmed that they'd kept the script that I forgot about the car for a few minutes. I cried as I read all of the personal notes my mother and father had written throughout the three-page document. Stapled to the back page was a picture of the three of us in the hospital when I was born. They'd made promises to themselves and to me long before I ever took my first breath. I thought about the life I once had. My parents didn't bend to trends but strived to do the best for their children. They provided a loving home overflowing with encouragement and support. Regardless of what happened the day before or the day after, they were perfect parents in that moment. As I read their words, I never thought they could do my heart any harm, and neither did I think they ever would.

    I smiled at my mother looking down at me in one of the photos. I still had that signed script, and deep down, I still felt that sentiment.

CHAPTER 5

VERA

A week had passed since the anniversary celebration, and I was still in shock. My father's once stately frame looked so frail beneath his loosely hung suit. His face had lost its fullness and his hands seemed smaller than I remembered.

He'd tried to reassure me that everything was okay but I knew something was off. He could smile and laugh for the guests, but I saw my father's likeness wasting away in front of me. Throughout the event, I stayed near his side, fearing something terrible would happen if I left him for a second. I was overreacting, but what else could I do?

When it came time for him to toast my mother, I winced as his voice was repeatedly broken by aching coughs and muffled groans. She fought to hold back tears as he promised to love her beyond the confines of time. Damien kept squeezing my hand as if to remind me to hold it together. The celebration lasted for a couple of hours, and he didn't want me emotionally breaking down at the dinner table. Regardless of what he wanted, seeing my father in that state left me heartbroken. I loved my mother, but we'd never found a solution for the chasm that existed between us. We were just too different. When I'd visit them, I spent more time sitting and talking to my father than her. We could debate politics, religion, and even discuss the antics of reality show celebrities. When I was younger, I doubted the need for a father. But now that I'd been fortunate to have an amazing one, I couldn't imagine my life without him.

Annie kept whispering questions in my ear about her grandfather's appearance. I didn't want to lie, but I didn't believe her young heart could handle the truth. Instead, I put on the same invisible mask my parents had worn for my benefit and comforted her with words of everything being okay.

When I went to visit them the following day, I was finally told the truth. My father had an aggressive cancer and a bleak prognosis. It was too late for chemotherapy, radiation, and any other alternative medication at that point. My parents had known for three weeks and hadn't bothered to tell me or anyone else. Aunt Sandy probably knew, but she was adept at holding a secret—especially life-changing ones.

After they told me, I asked several questions—some rhetorical, some not. I accused my mother of being selfish for not being honest sooner and I refused to look my father in the eyes.

"Vera, I'm not dead yet. Come over here and sit down so we can talk without all that yelling."

I don't know if a voice can be strong and frail at the same time, but his was. His message had the same strength as when I'd lost homecoming queen and wanted to drop out of high school. Or all the times I complained about my mother and threatened to run away. His words were firm but compassionate. I exhaled slowly as I took a seat next to him on the couch. Tears fell as I turned my body to face his.

"Your mother and I know this is tough to hear. We've had time to digest the news. But don't forget that while it's easy to question God, it's not what we do in this house. Human minds can't fathom how our small misfortunes factor into His master plan. It's God's call when we enter this world and God's call when we shall leave it. Peace and contentment are choices. I'm at peace regardless of what happens."

He put his arms around me, and I rested my head on his chest. Every time I tried to speak, the words got caught in my throat until I finally stopped trying. My mother sat down beside me, patting my knee while crying softly. Sometimes a touch far exceeds the words of a broken heart. It was almost an hour before either of us moved from the couch.

Vibrations sounded from the driver's side cup holder. Fortunately, I was still parked in the grocery store lot and could easily check the text message. It was Zoe wanting to know if I was still up for that evening's plan.

On the way home from my parent's house, I'd called her to tell her of our father's illness. I figured someone should break the news to her, and with his prognosis, it couldn't afford to wait. Zoe's response had been a few minutes of silence and then a muffled urgency to end the call. I didn't need to ask if she was okay, I knew she wasn't. Her feelings were just as confused as mine. Maybe putting all of the pieces together would be the best next step. Plus, I needed to clear my conscience. The flashbacks were occurring rather frequently, and the guilt was becoming unbearable. It was time to come clean before we all lost the benefit of time.

CHAPTER 6

YVETTE

"Let's go to the fair," Zoe said casually the following morning while making shrimp and grits.

"What fair?" I wasn't interested in going to one of those pseudo-fairs that takes place in a mall parking lot. The rides look flimsy, feel angry, and cost too much.

"The Georgia National Fair is in town, and it's Teacher Appreciation Week."

Zoe smiled in my direction. I knew my little sister pretty well, and I was guessing that she'd already purchased tickets and was asking only as a courtesy.

"You already have tickets, don't you?"

Her smile widened as she handed me a bowl and a napkin.

"I do! I remember how much we love going, and since it's been more than five years since you were here around your birthday, I figured we could go have some fun! Plus, I'm not spending my vacation week sitting in this house looking at the walls."

I gave her a look of annoyance, but when she looked back with hopeful eyes, I agreed.

"Speaking of walls, I like the changes you've made, especially the pictures of Mom in the guest bedroom," I said as I filled my bowl.

"Thanks! I decided to take some photos from the albums and actually put them to use. This way, people can remember how beautiful she was. If you look in my office, you'll see the one of us with our snowman.

"I remember our snowman! Wow, what year was that?"

"I have no clue. I just know it was the one time it snowed enough for us to build a snowman."

We laughed while remembering how surprising it was to wake up and find a few inches of actual snow on the ground. Our father had taken us outside and taught us how to make the perfect snowball.

"Did Mom ever come outside that morning? I remember her being nervous, but I don't remember if she actually called our bluff."

"Nervous? She was terrified! We threatened a full-on snowball attack. One step and she was a goner."

Tears from laughing so hard ran down my cheeks as memories of that day filled my head.

"Didn't we name him? I think it was something like Marvin or Marcus."

"Martin the Snowman. That's it! He was lopsided and had one good arm!" I stopped laughing long enough to take another bite of my french toast. Our neighbors were outside that morning playing in the snow as well. We took several pictures, mostly with lopsided Martin.

"Is the picture in your office the one with the two of us or the one with us and dad?" I asked casually.

"It's the one with the two of us," Zoe replied. She opened

her mouth to say something but closed it quickly.

"I noticed the new bathroom wall color. it's olive green, my favorite. I really like it!"

"Thanks, I thought about you when I picked the color. At first I was hesitant, but I think it blends with the earth tones throughout the house."

"C'mon let's go out and get some fresh air. I haven't been here in months. I'd like to see what's new in my hometown."

Zoe got up and took our plates to the sink.

"Well don't expect too much. In terms of "whelmness," you will be whelmed. Not underwhelmed, not overwhelmed. Just…whelmed," I burst out laughing as I handed her our drinking glasses.

"Still not impressed by the seventy-two steps, eh?"

"I'm just saying, it wasn't what I expected. I understand. Rocky ran up the steps in the movie and did the little two step at the top. But I felt *whelmed* when I saw them. There wasn't even a sign!"

"There was a sign, it said Philadelphia Museum of Art!" I playfully threw a dish towel her way.

When Zoe came to visit me in Philadelphia for the first time, I took her on a tour of the city. We saw the Liberty Bell, Love Park, Constitution Center, South Street, Penn's Landing, and the Art Museum. Oddly, she was most excited about the Rocky steps and felt somewhat let down when she finally stood in front of them. I wasn't certain of her expectation, but her degree of disappointment surprised me. To make up for it, I took her to see Philadanco at the Kimmel Center that night.

"They should've had a sign for the steps."

We both shook our heads while heading to our respective rooms to shower and dress.

We drove around for most of the day, looking at small changes in the neighborhoods. Zoe showed me the high school where she worked, and we discussed her job as a teacher. That she's able to work with teenagers is remarkable. It requires a level of patience I've yet to master.

I listened as Zoe vented about her students' lack of focus and accountability. But even though her words were frustrated, her voice was hopeful. Zoe wants the best for her students, and deep down, she still believes they can accomplish anything. I didn't chime in too much because I was less confident in their ability to get out of their own way. I dread Kayla crossing over into that territory as our interactions will likely shift from being rooted in mutual respect into something drastically different. I remember how arrogant and self-centered I was toward my parents once I hit my core teen years, and I don't want that type of relationship for us. I want Kayla to remain my little girl forever.

A regional bank sat in the location where our favorite discount movie theater once stood. I pointed toward the bank, and before I could say anything, Zoe interrupted and confirmed my fear. The old movie theater was gone, along with so many memories of our past. I reminded myself that things change. That still didn't stop me from being sad.

As we rode around, I grew more silent with each mile. I wanted to ask Zoe about her personal life. Only a year ago she was engaged and living with her fiancé, but apparently things turned sour not long after she said yes. She was devastated and didn't want to discuss the details, so I tried to respect her privacy. Now, with those memories in the rearview mirror, it seemed more acceptable to ask questions. But for whatever reason, I still hesitated.

Zoe's high standards were always apparent, but I sometimes wondered if her failed relationships were a direct consequence of our broken family. She's far less forgiving and understanding with the men in her life compared to her friends or even her students. She knows what she wants and has clear expectations but seems to consistently choose men who will never be able to meet them. Once, she dated a man that responded to a broken promise by saying, "Zoe, you are the type of person that actually expects people to do what they said they would do." She dated him for 6 months after that conversation! By the time her fiancé was introduced, I'd grown accustomed to smiling and nodding and not getting involved.

"So have you talked to Aunt Sandy recently?" Zoe asked while we were waiting on two fruit smoothies at a local dessert favorite. I decided to broach the subject of jilted lovers at another time.

"No, I haven't, and I just remembered she called my cell while I was in route yesterday. I'll call her when we get back to the house," I said as I made a mental note.

The Georgia National Fair is held annually in Perry, Georgia, at the agricultural center. It's a huge spectacle of animals, food, and rides that make the half-mile trek from the parking lot to the gate entrance well worth it. Growing up, we went every year, and one year, I even entered a watercolor painting in the pre-teen art competition. The competition was for eleven- and twelve-year-olds, and I was ten. I won fourth place. My parents were so proud of me, and I reveled in the attention. Because I was the youngest entrant, my fourth-place ribbon was a first-place victory in my eyes.

It took us thirty minutes to get from I-75 to the fair entrance. Luckily, we were in great spirits and knew it'd be well worth it. Plus, I was on a mini vacation with no concrete plans, so there was no rush. After we parked the car and stood in line to have our handbags checked for weapons and bottles, we were finally on the other side of the iron gates.

"Okay, what's first?" I looked at Zoe with excitement. We had about forty-five tickets, and I wanted to use every single one of them.

"Let's head this way and see if something jumps out at us." Zoe started walking to the left, and I fell in step. There were several people enjoying candy apples, freshly squeezed lemonade, and homemade peach cobbler. The smells were amazing, and I remembered why I love (and miss) Georgia so much.

"Are those boiled peanuts?" I smiled as I watched the man shovel three cupsful into a plastic sandwich bag. Not more than a week ago, a colleague and I were explaining, unsuccessfully, the flavor of boiled peanuts to a Midwesterner. I never realized, until that very moment, how difficult it is to explain the flavor and the process. My colleague looked somewhat disgusted as the two of us struggled to explain why people pay money to suck soft peanuts from a wet shell.

"Come back to get those. We need to start things off with a great first ride. What do you see?"

I looked around the fairgrounds, trying to get a glimpse of anything that would be considered "great" in Zoe's eyes.

"What about the Freeze?" I pointed to a ride about fifty yards ahead. We could hear loud, vibrant music blasting from the distant speakers. a long line of anxiously waiting people confirmed that the Freeze was the "it" ride of the night.

"Looks like something we should try!" Zoe said excitedly as she grabbed my arm and led me toward what felt like a treacherous fate. My nervousness grew with every step.

The Freeze was quite massive when compared with the rides on its opposite sides. White in color and modeled after what looked to be a chain of snowcapped mountains, The Freeze was a force. The name glowed in bright blue letters against the all-white backdrop. even though it appeared like other rides and only circled around one track, I noticed that half of the track was hidden behind a massive wall. As we approached, I thought to myself, this looks like a line full of eighteen-year-olds. I gave Zoe a questionable look that asked if we were really prepared to do this. I was far from a teenager, and so was she at thirty-six. But when I looked into her eyes, I sensed she was more than a little ready.

The knots in my stomach grew as we inched closer and closer to the front of the line. As the intensity of the music increased, so did my fear. After we gave the gate keeper our tickets, found two empty seats, and secured our safety bar, I remembered how much I disliked roller coasters. I don't mean having simply a small distaste for them. I mean more like a massive abhorrence. The thought of paying someone to take my body on an adventure of twists and turns that would leave me feeling nauseous and dizzy—and let's not forget the pounding headache—stopped appealing to me a few decades ago. I closed my eyes, laid my head back, and as the ride started its first spin, I thought, *I'm too old for this.*

Once I placed my feet solidly on the ground, I smiled. Zoe's comments as we exited confirmed she enjoyed the experience much more than I had. The Freeze was as uncomfortable as I had imagined, but it was brief, which I appreciated. I spent most of the time being surprised at the carefree nature of my little sister. She'd screamed louder than some of the teenagers. Her hands were in the air most of the time, and she was singing, loudly and off key I might add, to whatever top 40 hit they played. There was no chance of her smile fading, and it quickly became infectious. I actually liked it a bit more than I thought I would because of how much she'd enjoyed it.

"Wow, I think I needed that. Thanks, sis. that was the perfect first ride," I said to Zoe as we walked back toward the boiled peanuts stand.

"Good, because if you don't let loose a little, we're going to come back every night until you leave."

Zoe and I always have fun together. Even though there is a six-year age difference, we have a solid friendship. In some ways after our mom's death, I became more of a motherly figure for her, but over time, I realized that she sometimes offered that same nurturing and comfort to me.

After buying two bags of boiled peanuts, we continued our exploration. As we tackled more rides over the next hour, my only request was that we sprinkle in a few slower, more casual ones, to which Zoe obliged. Being surrounded by the lights, people, and sounds relaxed my entire body. Zoe and I walked and talked and realized how far from our twenties we were. Our bodies couldn't take the jerking and swinging as well as they once had.

As we exited the Fun House, laughing and wondering why we decided to go in, we heard a few voices yelling, "Miss Maxwell," from somewhere near the ride's entrance. The teenagers were eager to say hello to Zoe, and she smiled broadly, returning a bit of their enthusiasm. Zoe introduced me and we all exchanged a bit of small talk. I always felt proud of my little sister when I saw her interact with her 'kids' as she called them. they respected and loved her just as much as she loved and encouraged them.

While some people fall into careers, Zoe was destined to be a teacher. When we were little, she could be found in our playroom "teaching" to her class of invisible students. She taught, fussed, corrected, and praised them. She was always tough but fair. They received graded papers with notes on how they could obtain higher scores with a little focus and critical thinking. A few times, I went and sat in on a "class" and found myself unable to do anything but disrupt her lesson. It was bizarre, and I couldn't get beyond the reality of sitting there and having her talk to people that didn't exist. Now, I realize she was simply preparing for the life that lay ahead. She has her own classroom filled with students that want her guidance, lessons, and praise every day. She's living her dream.

As we walked toward the exit, my heartbeat quickened. Roughly fifteen yards ahead was one half of the collective "them." Initially, I'd received nonstop calls about his wife. My family and friends wanted to know how I felt about Mary, my stepmother elect—what I thought about her looks, clothes, job, and everything in between. At that time, I wasn't interested in discussing my father, the situation, and much less the woman that I sometimes thought was a catalyst for things going in the direction they had. How ironic that she is a marriage and family therapist but had done little to help repair the relationship between the man she supposedly loved and his daughters. As the years passed and Mary's daughter, Vera, grew from an innocent fifteen-year-old to the thirty-one-year-old woman standing a few yards away, she became the part of the pair on which everyone focused.

The slender 5'8" elementary school teacher walking within five yards of us was definitely beautiful. Her face revealed white teeth and patient eyes. Long strands of wavy, auburn hair gathered behind her ears and rested on her shoulders. I took in the tan crops, orange and green blouse, and brown sandals. A pair of 18-karat gold medallion earrings dangled from her ears, and a matching necklace adorned her neck. I could easily tell she had style and maybe if things had been different, we would've been shopping buddies.

"Hi, Zoe, Yvette," she said almost nervously. I looked at the girl who had received the gifts from a father I forfeited. Her biological father had been inconsistent and, based on grocery store gossip, abusive. Mary banished him from their lives long before her physical scars vanished, and any emotional damage had developed for Vera. For her, it must have been a gift to have my father come along. Even though he was strict, his kind nature would never allow him to hurt them. They needed security, and in most ways, he provided it.

"Vera, what a coincidence running into you! Yvette, isn't it great to see Vera?" Zoe embraced Vera with comfort and familiarity. I was surprised but tried not to show it. I instead smiled and nodded in her direction. It isn't that I have an issue with Vera, at least not anymore. I can't blame a child for an adult's mistakes. Although she has always been merely an innocent bystander, my heart hurts no less from the nights when I needed the father that was enjoying dinner at her table. Her very presence made it easy for him to walk away from us. Her existence gave him hope that he could create a new life and live a new reality. Why have two daughters that remind you of your imperfect past when you could be the perfect father to someone new?

I decided to check my phone for missed calls or texts from Christopher while they continued talking. Kayla was preparing for a big exam in her earth science class, and I wanted to remind Christopher to limit her television time.

"...it's just happening so fast and no one knows exactly what to expect," Vera said softly while releasing a deep sigh.

I wanted to care about her problems, but I couldn't find the sympathy to do so. The first time we met was right after Kayla's second birthday. We'd come down from Philadelphia for my cousin's high school graduation. The school was in a neighboring community, which had multiple high schools, and each graduation consisted of at least two commencement ceremonies, three hours apart. Ironically, the ceremonies were all held where we were standing at that very moment: the agricultural center. I'd been selected by my family to leave the comfort of the bleachers for the main floor. We were sitting pretty far from the stage and wanted a few up-close pictures of her receiving her diploma. While making my way down the steps, I passed two young women smiling and looking at the pictures they'd just taken. Vera and I passed one another with only a simple "excuse me," which had the awkwardness usually reserved for strangers and passersby. When I got back to my seat, Zoe looked at me, and I nodded. Afterwards, as we drove to the celebratory barbecue, I told Christopher. He was surprised to learn that I'd just met my stepsister face to face for the first time.

Back then, I didn't know how I should feel about seeing her or if I should have any specific feeling at all. When I saw pictures of her at Aunt Sandy's house the year before, there were pangs of jealousy. I'd almost been weakened to my knees. However, when we passed one another on the steps, the only thing I felt was relief.

"No, not yet, but I'm sure Yvette will keep you all in her prayers as well. She's in town for a week, so we'll see what we can do." I snapped out of my reflecting when I heard my name.

"Keep who in my prayers? I'm sorry, I must have missed something." I struggled to figure out what was said while I was reminiscing.

"Mommy! Mommy! Look at what daddy won for me!" We all looked in the direction of the voice. There was a 6'3" well-built man coming toward us with a giant pink bear in his arms. A few steps ahead, running excitedly toward her mother, was Vera's daughter.

Vera's face lit up as she reached for her daughter's hand and gave her husband a high five.

"Congratulations, sweetie. I bet it only cost a small fortune." She winked at her husband, and he grinned sheepishly and nodded. I'd never met Vera's family, and before this moment, not been inclined to do so. But seeing the three of them together reminded me of Christopher and Kayla and how much I love our little family moments.

"Yvette, Zoe, this is my husband, Damien, and my daughter, Annie. Well, it's actually Annette, but we call her Annie," Vera said.

"Nice to meet you both," said Damien. Zoe and I shook hands with Damien and returned the pleasantry. I looked down and saw Annie smiling up at me.

"Well, hello there, Miss Annie," I said playfully.

"Hi," she said as she stepped forward and took my hand. The gesture surprised me, but I didn't pull back. She slowly swung her arm, which caused mine to follow. It felt like being at the fair with Kayla when she was Annie's age. Annie talked about her favorite rides while I listened intently and asked questions.

Meanwhile, the other adults continued their conversation about how Damien had come to win such a big prize.

". . . and after the sixth try, I almost threw in the towel. At that point I could've bought her the bear outright for less money. But Annie insisted I keep trying, and my pride wouldn't let me disappoint her. Finally, on the ninth try, I won. It cost me about forty bucks, but watching her face light up when the guy handed it over made it all worth it."

I trickled in and out of both conversations, realizing that it was more natural than I would've assumed. if anyone was watching our little exchange, they'd probably think we were a happy family with shared memories.

At one point, I looked to my left and saw the three of them watching us.

"Your daughter is beautiful and very smart," I said to Vera with a smile. She thanked me for the compliment as Annie squeezed my hand.

"So, are you my auntie?" she asked innocently. I looked over to Zoe, not knowing what exactly to say.

"Yes, sweetie, we're your aunts," Zoe said without missing a beat. I saw Vera's chest fall from the heaviness of labored breaths. Without having to say a word, Zoe knew I was ready to leave the fair.

CHAPTER 7

VERA

Well, that wasn't a part of the plan. I looked at Damien and shrugged.

"Mommy why did my new aunties leave?" Annie looked at me with eyes that expected a simple answer.

"Annie, I'm not quite sure why they left but you'll get to see them again. okay?" I squeezed my daughter's nose in my hand and raised her chin so we were looking one another in the eyes. After a few seconds, I rubbed my nose against hers which always made her smile.

"Your nose is cold!" she said as she laughingly pulled away. I stood upright and looked at Damien again.

"You okay?" he asked.

"Yep, I'm fine. I doubt anyone knew exactly how that was going to go." I shrugged again and allowed him to take my hand into his.

"Well, we still have a few tickets left. Let's use 'em." Annie echoed her father's sentiment, and we continued walking around the fair.

Try as I might, I couldn't stop looking toward the entrance in hopes of seeing Zoe and Yvette. I'd been anxious for days thinking about what would happen when we were all together. I never expected it to be so brief. The intent was to start small with a little run-in at the fair and then possibly evolve to something more significant, like dinner. I'd talked to Zoe several times so I knew the biggest barrier would be Yvette. The woman hated me and no matter how friendly I tried to be, she'd always have a gripe with me. Throughout our ten-minute interaction, she barely looked at me and paid more attention to her cell phone than our conversation. I'm surprised she didn't ask about her own father's health. There he was fighting for his life, and she couldn't care less. She even pretended not to know who we were talking about! I knew she was selfish and that just proved it.

Maybe I didn't need to say anything. Whatever action I took all those years ago was justified. Yvette and Zoe had good lives. They were both successful and didn't really need a father anymore. Plus, they're the ones that turned away from him. All I did was accept him and try to make him proud. They'd spent years having the support of two parents, and I deserved to know how that felt. I wanted to have two people sitting in the audience at my high school graduation celebrating me, cheering for me. They'd both already known that feeling. I hadn't taken anything away from them that they hadn't already discarded. I deserved a father too.

"Vera are you coming?" I looked up to see Damien and Annie waiting for me by the carousel.

"Oh, yeah. Sorry," I smiled weakly as I slid through the open gate. Annie and I sat in the available tea cup while Damien figured out how to ride a horse and hold on to the bright pink bear. We quickly forgot about the carousel and instead laughed at Damien as he tried to maintain his balance while carrying Annie's new playmate. He was visibly relieved when the ride stopped.

"That carousel was going faster than normal!" He said somewhat out of breath.

"Umm, no. It went the same speed as any regular carousel for kids. I guess those hands aren't quite ready for the pros."

He looked at me and slowly extended his bottom lip. He poked it out like a disappointed five-year-old. I shook my head refusing to acknowledge his tactic. He looked so cute though and after a few seconds, I kissed him on the cheek as an apology.

"Okay, where to next?" I asked Annie.

"Well…" her voice trailed off as she looked around the fairgrounds.

The wind felt a bit chilly, and I regretted not having brought a sweater. It was much warmer when we left home but now the unseasonably warm weather had given way to a much cooler Georgia night. I glanced up into a clear blue sky filled with twinkling stars.

"I have an idea. If we leave now, maybe we can make hot chocolate when we get home." I looked at Damien surprised.

"With extra marshmallows?" asked Annie.

"Is there any other way?" responded Damien with a huge grin.

"Yay! I want hot chocolate and marshmallows!" Annie skipped around talking in a sing-song voice. Every time I'd start to forget how well he knew me, Damien would do something like this. He winked and I returned the gesture. I'd been ready to leave right after the debacle with my stepsisters, but I didn't want to ruin our family time. Plus, given the cooler weather, I was looking forward to a mug of hot chocolate as well. We started in the direction of the parking lot passing some of my students, current and former, along the way.

"When we get home, I'll fix the hot chocolate with Annie while you have some alone time. Maybe take a bubble bath or read a book, whatever you think would… help."

I wasn't sure how he knew but he could tell I still needed time alone with my thoughts.

I reached for the car door handle just as my cell started ringing in my handbag. My mother was frantic on the other end of the line. I settled into the car and quickly snapped in my seatbelt.

"Damien, they had to take my dad to the hospital. We have to go, now!"

CHAPTER 8

YVETTE

The next morning, loud vibrations disrupted my sleep. After a few slow blinks, it registered that the incessant noise was my cell phone. I glanced at the nearby clock to see 7:01 staring back at me. Expletives and moans filled my head, but my body simply reached for the phone.

"Yes?" Hopefully, irritation could be heard in both the word and the silence that followed it.

"Did you get my message?" It was my aunt. I'd forgotten to return her call yesterday, so this wake-up call may be a form of punishment.

"Yes, ma'am." I sat up and allowed my eyes to open fully. I could tell the call wouldn't be a quick one.

"Well, why didn't you call me back?" Apparently, my aunt's irritation trumped mine.

"Auntie, I apologize. Zoe and I spent all day yesterday catching up, and I planned to stop by today to visit you. Was it about something urgent?" I couldn't believe she was calling to chastise me for not returning a simple phone call. There had to be a reason.

"Well, what time are you coming over?" I caught the urgency in her voice, which caused me to sit up straighter. Several thoughts traveled through my mind as I paused before delivering a batter of questions.

"Is it something urgent? Do you need me to come over this morning? Are you okay?" I asked in less than ten seconds. Before she could answer, I headed to the bathroom to start the shower.

"No . . . well, yes . . . but we can discuss it when you get here." I stopped. I blinked. I panicked.

I told her I'd be over soon, and we hung up. The knot I'd felt on the plane returned and squeezed tighter. There were so many thoughts running through my mind. They all started and ended with the worst of emotions. I almost resented my aunt for doing this to me. I'd rather her tell me now and allow me to feel whatever I'm supposed to feel rather than taking me down a path of "guess the problem" for the next hour.

I kept telling myself nothing was wrong. She was a sixty-five-year-old woman, so everything was always urgent. But the voices in my head wouldn't stop reminding me of every call over the years I'd received from a family member or an old friend about someone dying or being on the brink of death. The conversations were always extremely awkward and made me feel violated. I never wanted to be angry or upset with the caller, but I found myself feeling that way. Their call had disrupted whatever peace I was enjoying and ultimately sent my emotions down a different path.

I slid a note under Zoe's door and grabbed a bottle of water before heading outside. As I looked at the empty driveway and remembered Zoe picking me up from the airport, I realized that, unlike most of my visits, I hadn't rented a car this time. I went back inside, grabbed Zoe's car key, and slid an updated note underneath her door. I paused briefly, trying to remember if she'd mentioned any morning plans. Once I felt certain I was in the clear, I quietly exited the house again.

As I drove to Sandy's, I replayed last night's run-in with Vera. Her husband was charming, and her daughter, Annie, was a little beam of sunshine. I began to smile but then felt a brief pang of guilt. *What do I have to feel guilty about?* The unplanned meeting had been awkward but also a relief. There had always been unanswered questions about his other side, and last night was the first time I had a chance to peer into their world without it being through third-party whispers or inconspicuous interactions.

Zoe had been uncharacteristically quiet after we left the fair. It wasn't until we were out of the parking lot and onto the interstate that she acknowledged what had happened.

"So, you're probably wondering what's going on with me and Vera…"

I nodded with a tilted head and raised eyebrows. I didn't speak because curiosity could be misread as judgment.

"Do you remember when I was selected by the Board of Education to participate in that twelve-week committee on bullying? I'm sure I talked to you about it. The group met for two hours every Tuesday night and Saturday morning."

I nodded that I remembered.

"What I didn't tell you was that Vera was also selected for it and we got to know each other and became cool. We have similar ideas on so many things beyond just the education system. Whenever we'd have breaks, we'd grab a snack and talk about the team's progress and other ways to make the program even better. On the last day, she asked if I wanted to grab lunch, and I said yes. That was probably a month ago, and this was my first time seeing her since then."

"So, considering we talk at least three times a week, you didn't think to tell me about this before now?" My voice was less loud and angry and more than a bit puzzled.

"What was I supposed to say? It isn't as if she and I go shopping together or anything. We worked together and during that time, got to know one another. Since the assignment ended, we've rarely talked."

"Rarely? So you two still communicate though?" I hated badgering Zoe for talking to her stepsister, but I couldn't pull the words back into my mouth, and as we kept talking, more feelings of betrayal surfaced.

"On occasion, yes, we still communicate. She might text me to see how things are going or vice versa. Sis, it really isn't a big deal."

"It *is* a big deal. To me, it's a very big deal. I can't believe you'd keep something like this from me. If we hadn't run into them tonight, would I still be in the dark?"

I didn't expect Zoe to answer the question, as it was more emotional than rational. I sensed her getting annoyed with my barrage of questions and subtle accusations.

"Tell me why it matters," Zoe said as she looked over at me.

"It matters because she represents everything that went wrong in our lives. Vera is the most glaring reminder of his mistakes. He chose them. He spent years providing for and protecting them. Every Christmas, birthday, Father's Day, he was with them. That's why it matters. He had decades to make things right with us, but he was too busy playing daddy to her."

"Yvette, I get it. I'm no stranger to our past. I know what he did, but we can't blame Vera for his choices."

I looked at her. Even though my words seemed coated in anger, I wasn't angry or even upset. I was more surprised by Zoe's naiveté. I shouldn't have to explain why fraternizing with Vera was a mistake. Zoe always had a soft spot at the wrong time and for the wrong people.

"I guess that's your choice," I said under my breath.

"On that, we both agree." She didn't look at me as she spoke, but I could hear the resolve in her voice. Her words brought our tense exchange to its end.

As I turned onto Aunt Sandy's street I tried to expel thoughts of last night from my mind. By the time I returned to the house, Zoe and I would be back on the right path and last night would be a distant memory.

Sandra Ellsworth is known as Aunt Sandy by both family and the neighborhood at large. She's a giving woman who knows how to settle a minor disagreement with logic and reason which makes her quite skilled at bringing people together. She volunteers at the local Methodist church, is a member of the city council, and has been a foster parent for twenty years. I have admired her throughout my childhood for knowing how to make adults understand the concept of listening to comprehend versus listening to respond. She's adept at spotting a lie from a distance and won't tolerate disrespect or inconsideration. She also believes people should only speak to improve upon silence, which makes nervous talkers embarrassed around her.

I usually visit Aunt Sandy during my trips to Georgia

because I know I'm her favorite niece. We drive around town with her asking nonstop questions about my work and life in Philadelphia and recent trips abroad that I've taken. Outside of Christopher and Zoe, she's my biggest supporter. Aunt Sandy makes me feel smart and special, and I never question needing a sense of validation from a maternal figure. At some point, she shouldered the responsibility of being my fill-in parent without a fight from me. We both allowed it to organically evolve, and only once did I think about the irony that she was my father's sister.

Aunt Sandy lives a few miles away in the Rose Lawn neighborhood. Over the past forty years, Rose Lawn went from being filled with local politicians to military families and contract workers largely due to the U.S. Air Force base built adjacent to our small town. With its great location and reasonable home prices, Rose Lawn was ideal for new families.

Sandy's house was located on a main street, allowing her to easily watch over her "flock." I smiled as I parked behind the jet-black convertible in the driveway. She's her own boss and somewhat of a free spirit. I imagined her cruising down I-75 with the wind blowing in her hair and her radio blasting a 1990s R&B hit.

Today, I found her relaxing in a rocking chair on the front porch. Her 1930s bungalow-styled house was forest green with white trim and large square columns across the front. The lawn was large, well-manicured, and ideal for her annual Juneteenth barbecue.

As I approached her, I noticed how integrated the gray and black strands were in her nicely coiffed hair. Her caramel skin had far fewer wrinkles than the average sixty-five-year-old, and she made no apologies for it. She wore a pair of dark blue capri pants, a yellow top, and a red belt. Some think Sandy is quite fashionable for her age, but I know age has nothing to do with it. She is an ageless beauty and time struggles to keep up with her.

"Now there is my precious Vet," she said as she stood to give me a long hug. Aunt Sandy is the only person on either side of my family that still refers to me by my childhood nickname.

I smiled back at her and after hugging for a solid minute, sat down in the remaining rocking chair.

"Would you like some iced tea?" She started pouring before I had a chance to decline. She handed me the glass and I took a sip. It was refreshing, delicious, and full of sugar, just how I remembered it.

I glanced over at my aunt as she sipped her tea and leaned back in the rocker. Her eyes had a faraway look, and her furrowed brow betrayed the smile on her lips. Her morning wakeup call came to mind and my heartbeat quickened.

"I've missed you, dear. How's everything in Philadelphia?" she asked without looking in my direction.

"Things are good. Kayla's doing her thing in school and has decided on yet another "career." This is the seventh one so far."

"That little girl has no clue what she wants to do because she's young and still needs to go through some things in life. She'll find her way eventually. Especially with all that energy and creativity she has. She reminds me a lot of you." Aunt Sandy smiled to herself.

"I can see that. Christopher and I don't push her toward or away from anything. We want to give her the benefit of figuring out some things on her own."

"How's Christopher?" Aunt Sandy's smile widened as she mentioned my husband's name.

"Speaking of figuring out a career, he's a little confused right now too. Lately, he's been struggling with the idea of going back into the classroom. He enjoys being a dean but misses his students."

"Well how do you feel about it?"

"Within five years, Christopher could be a college president, which is a big deal not just financially but professionally. I want him to be happy, so it has to be his decision. I'd love for him to achieve that in his career but that's my ego talking. As his wife, I'm gonna be supportive and trust his decision."

"That's good. As his wife you should always be his biggest supporter."

I nodded toward Aunt Sandy and took a sip of tea.

"My job is going really well. I changed my schedule so I can travel less and spend more quality time with Christopher and Kayla."

My aunt looked over at me, smiling as she patted my arm. "It warms my heart to hear how great things are for you, Vet. Even when you were a little girl, I knew you'd be successful. I'm so proud of you and still pleased that you allowed that man to be your husband."

I looked down at my wedding band and turned it around on my finger. A grin spread across my lips. Christopher didn't know it, but I almost turned down his proposal and walked away from our relationship. Mainly because I was confused and lost for so long that when something real and healthy presented itself, I didn't know how to digest it. At that point in my life, I couldn't fully comprehend a man standing before me offering such completeness.

Sandy is the only person that knows because hers was the door I knocked on late one Saturday night. I'd packed a small duffel bag, filled the gas tank of my Nissan Sentra, and headed south. I'd told Christopher I needed to take care of some things that weekend and I'd talk to him the following Monday. He looked surprised, considering he was still balanced on one knee with a ring in his hand. He looked up at me with dejection covering his face. He slowly shook his head with disappointment and hurt but agreed to meet on Monday.

After thirteen hours of driving, I stood at Sandy's front door with tears of confusion staining my face. She pulled me into an embrace and subsequently into the house. I told her, through sobs, about Christopher's romantic proposal and how much I loved him but that I was afraid to say yes. Although Sandy didn't quite understand my hesitation, I continued to explain and describe and sob. She simply pulled me into her bosom and held me.

My father had known me for my entire life and still chose to walk away from me. We had a connection, a bond, that was supposed to be the most powerful between two people. Yet, it wasn't enough to keep him from turning his back on me when I needed him the most. How could I trust that this man, Christopher, would be able to love me through any condition? He was promising me so many things, but hadn't my father also made promises? I said all of this to Sandy, and she listened intently.

I wanted to marry Christopher and start a family with him, but these questions and so many others kept me from responding with a certain and confident yes. I cried and cried, and Sandy just held on tightly. My tears weren't about the possibility of losing Christopher but because from the rejection I felt from my father. I suspect I went to Sandy's house for the same reason she wouldn't simply tell me what to do. She wasn't the type to interfere in matters of the heart, regardless of her personal beliefs.

"Yvette, I'm gonna tell you a story."

I looked at her with needy eyes and opened ears.

"When I was twenty-two, I met a young man named Oliver while working in my father's deli. He was so handsome and charismatic I fell in love at first sight."

She closed her eyes and smiled as she told the story. I could see her walking back in time and experiencing the smells and sounds from that scene so long ago.

"Oliver came into the store in his Air Force blues, and I almost melted into the countertop. His skin was a heavenly mocha that covered all 6'2" of his frame. His dark brown eyes quickly surveyed the deli before landing squarely on me. The curves of his mouth turned upward, and he exposed two cheeks with dimples and a line of straight, white teeth. My nervousness grew with every slow stride he took toward the counter.

When he was finally within reach, he introduced himself and kissed the back of my extended hand. From that moment forward, we were inseparable. He'd just been relocated to the nearby Air Force Base, working in aircraft engineering. He was twenty-five, an only child, and originally from Washington, D.C. Being in Georgia was a slight culture shock for him, but within a few months, he adjusted, and things were going well.

We had lunch at the deli every day. For dinner, I'd cook a good 'stick to the bones' meal. He accompanied me to family gatherings and even met you once, although it was some time later, and you were only a few months old. I doubt you'd remember. The family quickly took to him, and it wasn't long before rumors of him proposing surfaced.

I enjoyed the richness of Oliver's voice and never tired of his presence. I knew I loved him long before meeting him and I believe he felt the same way. That's how destiny operates. We were supposed to be together, and regardless of what obstacles were to come our way, we knew our love would win."

Sandy grew quiet, and I sensed her mood shift. Throughout my life, I'd never known her to be married. She'd had a few male friends, but nothing more serious than that. Before I could wrap myself in my own questions, she continued talking.

"Marrying Oliver was the happiest day of my life. The ceremony was held at St. Peter Missionary Baptist Church, right off of Highway 96. The majority of the town was there as weddings were a community celebration back then. Oliver wore a tailored black suit with a long, skinny blue tie and shiny, black wingtips. His smile almost glowed as I walked toward him in my white chiffon gown with beading at the top and throughout the train. I held tightly to the beautifully arranged bouquet of white calla lilies as I approached his side. "You look so beautiful," he whispered as we both turned toward the minister. Oliver was confident in his decision to have me as his wife, which made me even more comfortable with it. His hands were stable and gentle as he pulled back my veil and took me into his arms. We both committed our love on that day."

Aunt Sandy took a sip of her tea and wiped away a tear that threatened to fall.

"We were happy, Yvette. Do you hear me? That man and I were thrilled to be husband and wife. For three years we built a life together, shared our hopes and dreams and planned to start a family. I made him every dish I knew and then read cookbooks to learn how to make new ones. We volunteered together at the local shelter, and I saw how giving and sensitive he could be to the needs of others.

One day we received a letter in the mail. Oliver's squad was being deployed to Vietnam. While we always knew it was a possibility, we were heartbroken at the news. Oliver was gone a week later and I had no idea when or if he'd ever return."

I held Aunt Sandy's hand to keep it from shaking.

"Oliver and I sent letters constantly and I stayed close to the phone so I wouldn't miss his call. We went on like that for over a year. Then one day, two men came to my door. I recognized one as a friend of Oliver's from the Air Force. He handed me a letter, apologized, and saluted me before walking back to his car.

It took me two days to read the letter. I didn't want to face the truth that my husband was never coming home. What do people always say? It was as if my world had come crashing down. That's exactly how I felt. How could Oliver leave me? How would I continue living when the only life I wanted to live included him? I won't say it was easy, Vet, but day by day, I found the strength to move forward. I understood that just because things didn't go as I would have wanted, I was still blessed to have had Oliver in my life for those years. He was a gift to me, and I was a better person having known him. I'm not telling you what to do, niece, but I am telling you that you have to see the bigger picture. Don't reject the possibilities of your future because of the hurdles of your past."

I hugged Aunt Sandy and thanked her for being so open with me. I didn't ask for details about Oliver's final letter to her because I knew it would be too painful. He must have been a great man, and I was sad I didn't get to witness them together.

I kept thinking about her story as I got up from the couch. Sandy usually agreed with most of my decisions, so I knew she was concerned I'd make the wrong one. I understood her message, but I still needed to process everything, and I wanted to do it alone.

Aunt Sandy poured me a cup of hot tea, ran me a bubble bath, and gave me some space. I sat in those bubbles for hours playing back years of my childhood and all of the good and bad memories. I thought about every Christmas, birthday, family vacation, and so on. I saw photos with stilled smiles and unburdened hearts. My mind raced through the words of encouragement and advice offered by parents who cared about my well-being. I smiled at thoughts of my father teaching me how to drive and his look of pride as I was handed my driver's license.

Once the water turned cold and the bubbles had all but disappeared, I exited the bathroom and headed to the small bedroom at the back of the house. Aunt Sandy had turned down the bed and left a cup of chamomile tea on the nightstand. I loved that particular room because it had pictures of family, friends, and strangers on every wall and told of her history—our history. I stood in the middle of the room, glancing around while listening to the untold stories. Faces I'd never seen smiled back at me with a certain familiarity. People I'd never meet were posing in their Sunday 's best and seemed to be peering deep into my soul. There was one picture I hadn't noticed before. It was Aunt Sandy and a tall man standing in front of her father's deli. She wore a solid print sheath dress and black pumps. Oliver, in his dark dress slacks and short-sleeved shirt had his arm around Sandy's waist. Their faces exposed a happiness and joy only reserved for those that were destined to be together—those that celebrated lifetimes of love.

I don't remember when I stopped crying, but eventually, I did. I stopped feeling sorry for having a man in my life that loved me and wanted to share a forever kind of happiness. I stopped feeling pitiful and afraid because I knew I was resilient enough to endure. The situation with my parents taught me that I was strong. Oliver, Aunt Sandy, and every person in those photos were a testament to my strength.

The next morning, I hugged Aunt Sandy and thanked her for her guidance. I went back to Philadelphia, straight to Christopher's, and told him yes.

CHAPTER 9

YVETTE

"Yet, your father is dying."

She looked at me with eyes that knew my struggle. My aunt saw what my lips wouldn't commit to saying. I wanted to feel so many things, but I couldn't identify one single emotion. It was a confusing situation that deserved a heartfelt response, but I couldn't offer what seemingly didn't exist on the inside. I wasn't sad. I wasn't heartbroken. I wasn't angry. I was…indifferent.

I sat back in the rocker and sipped my tea without looking at my aunt or saying a word. Regardless of my indifference, he was still her younger brother. I knew how delicate this situation was, and I refused to take her on my rollercoaster of thoughts. Vera's comments from the previous night flashed through my mind. Zoe knew and didn't tell me. I'd wondered why she was so fixated on keeping in touch with Vera. We hadn't been concerned with talking to her before, so why now. I guess our father dying had changed things—at least in her mind.

"You still can't forgive him, can you?" Aunt Sandy didn't need an answer because deep down, she already knew. I continued looking out into the neighborhood as she tried to manage our two warring emotions.

"Yvette, I love you and want what's best for you. I've held my tongue for years because I thought it best not to interfere. But I can't continue being quiet because I'm afraid you're gonna make a terrible mistake. Wisdom is not given, it's earned. Sometimes by making mistakes and having regret. Do you want to live with this kind of regret?"

I digested her words carefully. Without turning my head, I flatly stated, "To think I'd have feelings of regret in the future assumes I have certain feelings for him now."

As I cautiously turned to look directly at my aunt, I knew she was taken aback by my lack of care or concern. By her thinking, the imminent threat of death should soften even the hardest heart of stone.

"Yvette, I can't make you feel anything for your father, but I can remind you that he *is* your father. I know he hasn't been perfect, but he did the best he could."

"Well, clearly his best wasn't good enough." I blurted the response so quickly and forcefully that it surprised us both.

Sandy exhaled deeply as I stood and headed toward the edge of the porch. There was a tall Japanese maple tree I always considered exceptionally beautiful. The burgundy leaves were vibrant and alive against the autumn weather. I reached for one of the leaves and held it gently. Everything around me was overflowing with life, but in contrast, I was facing the truth that my father was losing his. I wanted to care, but time had taught me that allowing him any outpouring of emotion was against my best interests—my emotional stability.

It took a second to register my aunt's voice behind me.

"…in ICU at the regional hospital. It's stage four

prostate cancer. It doesn't look promising, Vet."

I turned around. Everything was unclear. I blinked a few times to help focus my vision. Stage four. Cancer. I had heard those words years before. My thoughts blended together.

"I have to get Zoe's car back, Aunt Sandy. Thanks for the tea." I rushed the words out as I hugged her and descended the steps. I needed to think. I needed to breathe. I needed to be alone. It was all too much for me.

"Vet, he asked me to tell you. He wants to talk to you and Zoe. He needs to talk to you girls." She tried to appeal to my heart.

I stood at the car door for a minute before looking back at her. I didn't say anything, but she saw the anger in my eyes. How dare he ask us to give him what *he* needs? Did he consider our needs over the last sixteen years? Did he console us or shelter us when we found ourselves struggling through a world without a mother? No, instead he chose to raise someone else's child and give her every bit of love and support that should've been reserved for us. He'd made that choice, not me. It had been years since we last saw one another, and I was supposed to care about him and his well-being?

"Zoe and I ran into Vera last night at the fair and I met her husband and little girl. She has a beautiful family, reminds me of Christopher and Kayla."

"What exactly did Vera tell you?" Sandy fidgeted a bit. A brief look of agitation showed on her face that I couldn't quite read.

"She didn't tell me anything. But it was actually a relief to finally put more than a name and face to the person that's been my replacement all these years. A woman that received all the benefits of the father I once believed I had. By the looks of it, he did a hell of a job."

Tears fell as I spoke. Sandy put her hand in her front left pocket and opened her mouth as if to speak but instead closed it. Our eyes met as tears welled.

"Please tell my now remorseful father to call Vera if he wants to talk. They've apparently spent years having father-daughter conversations, why stop now." I got in the car and left without another word.

My indifference had become resentment. It was his fault we had to exist in this way. It was his lack of thought or consideration that precipitated this whole situation. And now I was supposed to forget everything that happened and just give him what he wanted, what he needed. My mind wandered back to that fateful day, when he shrugged away our memories. I'd bottled up my hurt and stored it away for so many years. Now, with this news, there was a threat of it surfacing. Everyone wanted me to be the bigger person, but I had already done that. Instead of crying in a corner for months on end, I acknowledged that I had lost my father. I buried him emotionally and mourned his loss before marrying Christopher because I knew I couldn't be a whole woman to him while having a burdened heart. I said my prayer and walked away. I couldn't be forced to relive something that almost destroyed me.

As I left Sandy's, I grew increasingly upset. I grabbed my cell phone and called Christopher, hoping he wasn't out with Kayla and unable to talk openly. He picked up on the second ring. Before we could get into the general pleasantries, I told him about last night's run-in with Vera and the morning wakeup call from Sandy.

Christopher listened and gave the occasional "okay" or "uh huh." When I got to the part about my father dying of cancer, he released a soft "wow." I wrapped up by venting about my feelings and how unfair it was for me to have to deal with this man after everything he'd put me through.

"Yvette…I know you're upset, but maybe you need to slow down and think about this decision. You say you're not angry with him but that's not how it sounds. Your dad is dying and wants to talk to you. Don't you think that counts for something?"

"Excuse me?" I asked flatly.

"Life is short. You know that better than anyone. What about Kayla? Doesn't she deserve to meet her grandfather and get to know him? What about her having a relationship with Annie? She's her cousin."

My right foot almost slammed on the brakes. I couldn't tell if I was suffering from disbelief or if I was wildly upset with the words coming out of my husband's mouth.

"Christopher, are you serious? Have you forgotten everything I told you? Why should I let him hurt Kayla in the same way he hurt and disappointed me?"

Part of me knew I didn't truly fear my father hurting Kayla. However, I what's the benefit of introducing her to someone on his deathbed? Isn't that setting her up for pain? I ignored the part about Kayla and Annie forming any kind of bond. I had to focus on the issue at hand: my father.

Christopher was trying to help, but how could he not understand my unwillingness to bend on my feelings? It's amazing how much we forget when someone is about to die or has died. They all of a sudden become faultless. We forget the lies, deceit, hurt, confusion, and destruction the person caused. Why? I can't understand it. My father isn't a horrible man, but he decided he wanted to be selfish and focus on his needs rather than the needs and wishes of his children. I'm not saying that the town should stone him or anything. I'm just saying as the child that was disregarded and emotionally discarded, I shouldn't be forced to forget his wrongs against me.

Christopher spoke with patience, but he disagreed with my feelings.

"Sweetheart, I love you, and I will always be here for you. I'm only trying to give you a different perspective. A lot has happened over sixteen years, and you don't know where that man is in his emotional journey. Maybe he finally understands what he put you girls through and it's time to make that wrong, right. I don't want you to regret not giving him that chance."

I listened to his words with intent. He was the second person to mention regret.

"Christopher, let me call you back. I love you."

I needed to think, and while I appreciated his honesty and perspective, this was personal.

Christopher and Sandy wanted me to be open-minded, and while my heart felt like giving in, I couldn't. It was settled. I drove to the cemetery and cried at the foot of my mother's grave.

CHAPTER 10

YVETTE

Zoe was seated at the dining room table eating a bowl of cereal when I walked into the house.

"Hey," was all I said as I walked past her and into the living room.

"I guess Aunt Sandy told you."

I slowly turned toward Zoe and looked at her with a hint of confusion and surprise.

"Told me what?"

"What I've been fighting not to tell you for the past twenty-four hours," she said while looking up from her bowl. "I wanted to but Sandy asked me not to. She knows how you feel, and she wanted to try to reason with you or something. Maybe see if she could change your mind."

I searched her face for…something. I'm not quite sure what I wanted to see in her eyes, but I knew I was searching.

"Change my mind about what?" I sat down across from Zoe at the table and put my head into my hands.

"About going with me to the hospital."

Zoe was being way too casual about the situation. These were very important sentences that were being thrown out with ease.

I lifted my head and eyed her for a few seconds. Her expression was difficult to dissect. She didn't look shocked or angry or sad. I shook my head slowly, lowered it, and finally allowed it to rest again in my hands.

"Yvette, it's easy for you to write him off and go on about your day. You live a thousand miles away. You won't run into him at the grocery store or see him while you're out enjoying a movie. I've spent decades trying to avoid and dodge and hold a grudge, but I'm done with the nonsense. It's tiring, and I don't know how someone spends so much energy despising another person so much. What has to happen for this emotional war to be over? Does the suffering end when he dies, because it looks like that's just around the corner."

Zoe's words came at me with sharp edges and subtle strength. I wanted to yell answers to her questions, but I knew they were rhetorical. In my mind, there was no ending to something that no longer existed. Strangers don't need to say goodbye because there's nothing that'll be missed between them. I didn't know the man that sat in that hospital room because he voluntarily removed himself from a life that included me. That was his choice, and he made it years ago.

I got up from the table.

"So, you don't have anything to say?" I couldn't tell if she was hurt or bothered.

I stood with my back to her for what felt like days but was probably only a few seconds. I turned around feeling the weight of our situation on my shoulders. Our eyes met, and then mine quickly retreated. I was emotionally spent.

"Zoe, there's a lot I can say, like how upset I am with you for not telling me before today. I can say I feel like an inconsiderate jerk for not knowing last night when we ran into Vera. I hate having people feed me information on their timing because they think they know what's best for me. Do you know how betrayed I felt last night and now today? That man is dying, and everyone knew but me. I don't know what to say, but I can say with certainty I feel things for which words don't currently exist."

"Things just happened so fast. I didn't know he was going to be on his deathbed when I first planned this."

"Planned what?" I looked at my sister confused.

"I planned for us to run into Vera at the fair. I wanted you to meet her family and maybe for us to all hang out in a non-threatening environment." Zoe's hands moved around as she spoke adding a bit of animation.

"You basically partnered with Vera to set me up?"

"No…yes…maybe," Zoe's voice trailed off as she sighed deeply.

"I just wanted to end the drama. But a few days ago when I spoke with Vera, I found out dad was in the hospital. I considered canceling the plan, but doesn't it make even more sense now? Vera's our stepsister and our father is dying! You and I have gone through this before. We know how hard it is to go to sleep because that might be the night your parent doesn't wake up. She has no idea what's about to happen, but we do. Maybe in helping her we can help ourselves. Don't you get that?"

A huge weight rested on my mind and heart. It grew with the conversations of the day. I was drained. All of this was far too much to process. Zoe didn't try to stop me from leaving the room, although I know she expected me to give a passion-filled retort. It just wasn't in me. My day started with an abrupt call followed by a shocking piece of news. I simply wanted to get under the covers and go to sleep. So I did.

CHAPTER 11

VERA

I surveyed the image staring back at me. My hair was disheveled and my eyes red and exhausted from crying. Tiredness caused me to collapse onto the bench at the end of the bed. The woman in the oval shaped mirror looked as dejected as I felt.

I'd been going back and forth to the hospital, and it was taking a toll on every part of me. Annie was at a neighbor's house playing with friends. Damien was at the gym, and I was supposed to be taking a nap before meeting with Zoe later that afternoon. Light emanated from under the bathroom door. Damien must've left it on. I slowly went over to flip the switch. I wanted nothing more than to be surrounded by total darkness.

I went to the bathroom but instead of turning off the light, I stood in front of the sink. The image in that mirror was even more unrecognizable. I pressed my waist against the countertop and leaned towards my reflection with my upper body. Dark circles had formed under my eyes and my lips were dry and chapped. I frowned at myself.

I opened the cabinet in search of facial cleanser and

moisturizer. I had to pull myself together before heading to the coffeeshop. Plus, I didn't want Annie coming home to find her mother looking disoriented. She'd been to the hospital with us earlier that morning. She was smart and knew her grandfather wasn't well. Sandy suggested sending her to play with friends for the rest of the day since the visit had been a tough one. At first, I hesitated. I didn't want Annie out of my sight. But after prodding from Damien and Sandy, I agreed. They were probably right.

As I reached for the cleanser, a box of pregnancy tests caught my eye. With everything that'd happened since the anniversary celebration, a possible pregnancy had slipped our minds. I sat the cleanser beside the sink and removed one of the foil wrappers from the box. I tore along the perforated line and pulled out the white plastic object. There wasn't a need to read the instructions. I knew what to do. I stared at the test in my hand.

What if I'm pregnant? What if I'm not? Should I wait for Damien?

I sat the test on top of the bathroom counter and went back to washing my face. While brushing my teeth, combing my hair, and applying my makeup, I kept glancing at the test, not sure if it was fear or hope directing my eyes and filling my head. Finally, I couldn't take it anymore. After pulling off the plastic cap, I lifted the toilet lid and sat down. I had to know if I was pregnant, and I needed to know *now*.

After I was done, I re-capped the stick and placed it on the countertop. I watched the warm, soapy water cascade over my hands knowing that in a couple of minutes, I'd have my answer. But it didn't take minutes. Within a matter of seconds, a plus sign appeared in the small window. I delicately picked up the stick with my right hand and stared at the image. Every emotion imaginable swept over me. I looked up to find Damien's face looking back at me in the mirror. I hadn't heard him come in. We both stood frozen as the symbol darkened in color.

I stepped backwards and let my body fall against the bathroom wall. I slid down until I was settled on the floor. Damien sat down beside me, not taking his eyes off the plus sign.

"Vera, say something."

But I didn't know what to say. We'd been wanting this news for the past few months so I knew I should be happy, but I wasn't. I wasn't sad either. I was confused.

"Damien, I…" my voice trailed off.

"Aren't you happy? Shouldn't we be excited about this?"

The hurt in his voice was palpable.

"Yes, yes, we should be happy honey. I'm not saying I'm unhappy. I'm just confused."

"Confused about what?"

He scooted closer to me on the floor and took my body into his.

"I don't know and that's the problem. I'm stressed out, drained, anxious. It's like a constant fear that the bottom is about to fall out or something. I can't explain it because it doesn't make a lot of sense even to me. All the what-ifs that plague my mind sometimes don't even have a basis for being there. Now I just found out I'm pregnant at the same time my dad is dying. What if something happens to my mom or to you?"

Damien consoled me while listening to my broken sentences and sobs.

"Damien, I've spent years protecting my family and I'm afraid of losing it. All of it."

He put his hand on my stomach and turned me to face him.

"You can't keep thinking that way. Sometimes we lose people sweetheart. That's a part of life. It's not the prettiest or the easiest part but it's the one guarantee. Regardless, you are strong and we can get through this together. Like you always say, we can't allow fear to paralyze us."

"I know. It's so much easier said than done."

"Now you're carrying our baby boy or girl and the same way we give Annie the love and support she needs, we're going to do that for this little one. Whatever happened in the past is in the past. We've gotta keep moving forward."

With that, he kissed me on the forehead and pulled me into his chest. He was right. I had to find a way to move forward and stop holding onto old scars and childhood fears.

We sat in silence for a few minutes until I finally said, "Thanks. I love you."

"Anytime and I love you, too."

"So, it looks like we're having a baby."

I turned around and kissed him on the lips and for the first time that day, I smiled.

CHAPTER 12

YVETTE

My nap wasn't one of rest but of turmoil. I tossed and turned and finally gave up. I couldn't tell if there were too many thoughts swirling around my head or if I'd subconsciously refused to turn my brain off. *Why should I care about this man? Why should I care about his last wishes? I shouldn't. Should I?*

My physical struggle was as real as the internal one. I sat up in bed and stared at the mirror. My mental anguish was evidenced by a furrowed brow and down-turned smile. I knew this Yvette, and I knew her well. She was the mild-mannered one. The one that internalized everyone else's emotions and feelings, rarely communicating her own frustration or annoyance. She was there when tough decisions needed to be made and no one else had the nerve to make them. I spent many days wondering if whatever situation she was in would be the one that would break her. I brushed away the thought as thinking in third person had to be unhealthy. Plus, given the challenges I'd already endured, I was strong enough to handle just about anything. I knew I could push through.

I exited the room, leaving behind any thoughts of uncertainty about the situation. Zoe had left a note on the kitchen counter. She must have left while I was taking my pseudo-nap.

Yvette, I have to take care of a few things, but I should be back in a couple of hours. Please forgive me for betraying your trust. I'm going to the hospital tomorrow morning. I hope you join me.
—Love 'Z'

I reread Zoe's note, having already decided to go to the hospital. Try as I did, I couldn't really comprehend her actions. After years of me talking to him following mom's death and trying to mend fences, how was it that Zoe was considered the most forgiving? I was the one who dealt with him and his attorney. I had to hear the rejection in his voice while she had the privilege of being a student. She walked freely into this house while I had the battle scars from fighting to keep it. I shielded her from the brunt of his dismissal, which made it easier for her to forgive.

When our mom got sick, Zoe was a sophomore in college. I had just graduated with my MBA and started a new job at a consumer goods company. At first, we didn't understand the severity of the situation because our parents kept it from us. For an entire month, they held the secret of her sickness. Technically, they didn't know it was cancer. They just knew she was vomiting constantly and had torturous headaches. They had no idea how quickly the cancer would overcome her body. It spread with no prejudice. Brain tumors overtake their victims with little effort but high effectiveness. Our mother's constant vomiting, pain, and fatigue were not revealed until a doctor mentioned the words tumor and hydrocephalus—excess cerebrospinal fluid in the brain—after an examination. I immediately took a short leave of absence from my new job and considered several Georgia hospitals my home for the next two months. I was there for every operation and every post-op exam. I knew everyone at the neurology desks and had learned how to sleep somewhat comfortably in a hospital waiting room. I asked questions and then did online research to get the layman's details doctors failed to provide. I'd thrown myself into my mother's care. I brushed and flossed her teeth, washed her body, took her to the bathroom, and changed her sheets when the nurses took too long to respond.

One night while asleep on the couch in my mom's hospital room, I heard a loud thud. My mom had tried to go to the bathroom alone and ended up falling to the floor. When I asked her why she didn't just wake me up so I could help her, she looked at me with sad eyes and said she didn't want to bother me. In her mind, she was becoming a burden. In my mind, she was my mother and deserved all the care and attention she needed. I put her arm around my neck and slowly walked her to the bathroom.

Zoe didn't have those moments because instead of spending nights in the hospital, she was in her dorm studying for finals. My mother wanted to protect her from the ugliness of the illness, as well as make sure she focused on her studies. Education had always been a key priority in our household. So while I remember pill schedules and being covered in bile when I didn't grab the bucket quickly enough, Zoe only remembers the very end. Neither of us had it better. I got to spend the last two months of my mother's life by her side, but that meant seeing her at her weakest and most vulnerable. It meant being left with distorted images of her beauty and her mind.

My father was beside her as well over those final two months. Sometimes I wondered if he ever considered this tragic outcome. Did he ever allow his heart to accept the possibility of her death? He thought he could save her. He fed her and comforted her while clinging to the hope that God would heal her weakened body. His voice carried prayers of obedience and honor to God while his hands brushed her hair or massaged her hands. He wondered which day would be her miracle moment when she'd wake up recovered. My father thought he could save my mother, but that day never came.

Even with those thoughts adding confusion to my mind and conscience, I knew Zoe was right about going to the hospital. I smiled at the growth of my little sister. We somehow switched places over the past decade, and she was teaching me how to love beyond limits. I wanted Zoe to be right. There was a heaviness associated with the feelings I'd developed for our father and even Vera, but I couldn't just let my feelings go. Wouldn't that be a betrayal to my mother and her memory? I know she never wanted him to abandon us. He not only failed us, he also failed her.

I'd go to the hospital because I wanted to tell him just that. He had to know he'd traded a lifetime of great and settled for a life of insufficient good. Bitterness enveloped my heart as I considered everything I wanted to say. He needed to remember why he left us. He prioritized other people—congregations, neighbors, extended family, and a new wife and daughter. He had to admit how shortsighted he'd been, how little he fought for his family. I wanted to say simply that regardless of whatever lie he created as his new reality, he would always be a failure in my eyes.

CHAPTER 13

VERA

"I'd like two small green teas."

I offered a few crumpled bills to the perky teenager behind the register. Miniature bells on the coffeehouse door chimed as Zoe walked in and scanned the room of strangers until her eyes settled on me. I waved and pointed to an empty table in the far-right corner. She nodded and headed in that direction. After the smiling teen handed me the change and teas, I joined her.

"Hey, thanks for agreeing to meet," I said while placing both cups down and taking a seat.

"Oh, it's no problem. I'm sure you've had your hands full between Damien, Annie, and visiting the hospital." Zoe awkwardly smiled. Her voice sounded as tired as my body felt. She took a sip of the tea and closed her eyes as she swallowed.

"This is so good. Thanks Vera."

"You're welcome." I considered telling her about the pregnancy but decided against it. It was too early and besides, there was a hint of tension between us. We hadn't been face-to-face since the fair debacle and all our phone calls and texts had been limited to the rare moments when Yvette wasn't around.

The worsening of dad's condition increased my feelings of guilt of the mistake I'd made years before, but I was afraid of jeopardizing the relationship I'd recently built with Zoe. She'd never trust me again and neither would Yvette.

"Are you going to the hospital to see him?" I asked cautiously. Wanting to be respectful of Zoe's feelings, I'd avoided putting any pressure on her to visit Dad or even make a phone call. However, every day felt as though he'd slipped away even more than the one before.

"I'm going in the morning. Hopefully Yvette will stop being stubborn and join me."

"He definitely wants to see you. He's been pressuring Aunt Sandy to use her powers of persuasion to get you both out there."

"Yeah, I know. She's called a few times. Honestly, I don't have a problem with going to the hospital. I'm trying to let go of any and all negativity from my past and that includes this stuff with him. But Yvette, well, that's another story."

"I try not to pry but I don't understand what happened to tear you guys apart. Did you really go sixteen years without speaking because he wanted to sell your mom's house?"

"What? No. That's definitely not what all of this is about. At least not for me."

"Oh? So, what happened?"

"He changed. When I was little, my mom and I were extremely close while Yvette was more of the daddy's girl. Of course our parents loved us equally but there was something special about my relationship with Mom. We'd go shopping together and get our hair and nails done. We laughed at the same jokes and she always knew exactly what to say to make me feel better. Yvette wasn't a tomboy but she knew more about changing a flat tire and making a jump shot because she spent a lot of time with Dad and that's the stuff he taught her. They had their own special bond."

Zoe looked down at the cup of tea between her hands.

"Then mom got sick and went into the hospital. Week after week she's going through operations and tests and I was told to focus on schoolwork. They were trying to protect me but that's not how it felt. It felt like I was pushed out. No one told me what was going on and by the time classes had ended and I was able to be there every day, she was almost gone."

"She was forty-two. Forty-two! We didn't expect to lose her to cancer. How could I lose my mom when I still needed her so much?"

I held Zoe's right hand between mine. She wasn't crying but there was considerable emotional weight in her words.

"After she died, I couldn't breathe. It was as if the world had swallowed me whole. Everything I'd once cared to do, felt foreign and all too familiar at the same time. Everything reminded me of her. I spent months pretending to be okay while knowing I was anything but. I even considered dropping out of school. Fortunately, Yvette changed my mind. She stepped in and helped me find my strength. We tried to talk to dad, but he'd become cold and distant. A few weeks after the funeral, he was great. But then something happened and he just shut down. He spent all his time either in his bedroom or gone altogether. He didn't ask if we were okay and honestly, I doubt he cared."

I was surprised because I'd always assumed the girls had caused the friction. The man in our household had been loving and kind. I never would've expected him to turn his back on anyone, especially his grieving children.

"I'm sure he cared Zoe. He's your father."

She looked up from her cup and raised her eyebrows.

"Only he knows if he cared. What *we* know is he was married and raising you a short while later."

She pulled her hand back from mine and took a sip of tea. I couldn't tell if she'd become upset with me or just uncomfortable with being so emotionally exposed.

"Our parents weren't dating when your mother was alive, believe me," I said defensively.

"That's not what I'm implying. What I'm trying to do is help you understand why we weren't interested in being a big, happy family when you came along. I want it to be clear why Yvette finds it difficult to welcome you with open arms. There were too many wounds still open. Our family should've healed before he brought you and your mom into it. I was nineteen and motherless. How the hell did he think it was okay to leave me fatherless too? I never expected a miracle, Vera. I just wanted my dad."

I nodded a response as I didn't know what to say. Zoe's words and behavior proved there were years of hurt still dormant. There had been too many assumptions and not enough communication. I felt a wave of guilt as I realized just how much I'd helped widen the chasm between my sisters and my father.

CHAPTER 14

YVETTE

The next morning, Zoe was surprised to find me sitting on the couch, fully dressed and with my handbag in tow.

"So does this mean you're coming to the hospital?" Her expression read as a mix between surprise and confusion. I stood and exhaled at the same time, nodding in her direction.

"Yvette, this is good for you. It's good for us."

I shrugged.

The short drive to the hospital consisted of Zoe trying to fill the silence with random conversation about politics and community news. I listened mostly, not able to contribute because my mind was bundled in layers of thoughts. I wanted to be as open-minded as Zoe, but I couldn't. I couldn't quite let go of the past.

The hospital was less than fifteen minutes from the house, providing little time to think. Since the visitor lot was almost full, we spent the next few minutes driving behind a middle-aged woman carrying several balloons that read "Get Well Soon" and pushing a young child in a wheelchair. The boy looked around, smiling, ready to jump out of the small contraption at any second.

"Aww, he must've been released today. I guess there are happy endings." Zoe looked over at me offering a quick nod and shrug.

"I don't know how happy it is though. He's in a wheelchair and could be for the rest of his life. We don't know what happened or how it will affect him," I offered bluntly.

Zoe frowned at my response. I was definitely raining on her parade.

As we watched the woman and young boy, a car backed out of its space, opening a spot near the main door. We parked, and I again reminded myself that I didn't have to go inside.

The hospital was comprised of three buildings. The main building towered above the other two and was the most imposing. In the front, it had four beautifully sculpted ionic-styled columns. An American flag was posted near the entrance along with a placard with some historical information including the hospital's founding date.

Zoe must have felt my uncertainty because she started giving me a pep talk as we exited the car and walked toward the door. I glanced up at the main building and then at the adjacent structures. The other two buildings flanked the main building on either side. They were long and had windows every few feet. A woman in a hospital gown stared at us from one of the windows.

The main building looked new, as if recently remodeled. The side buildings looked worn, like the bricks would slide apart at any second. It was a physical depiction of my internal feelings.

A woman wearing a floral top and light blue pants greeted us at the registration desk. Zoe gave her our father's name. I stood quietly as the nurse looked at a computer screen, searching the database for a match.

She smiled at us after only a few seconds and pointed down the narrow hallway to the left while saying a three-digit room number. Zoe thanked her before we headed toward the room.

My feet were leaden, dreading each new step. In my head, conversations that never happened were blending with the ones that had. I wanted a perfect visit—a perfect conversation. Zoe abruptly stopped, and I realized we were standing at his door.

From the slightly open doorway, I could hear him talking to the television. He was watching one of those shows where someone preaches for thirty minutes, and then asks you to buy their new DVD, CD, or book. I could picture him sitting in the hospital bed with his arms raised and eyes closed, reciting the words on the screen. At this point, .they come naturally for him. It's all so effortless.

Years ago, my mother was sitting in a hospital bed, and he was watching a similar channel. Regardless of how much she told him the television was causing more pain because of the noise or because it hurt her already weak eyes, he kept it on. He wanted her to be reminded of her faith and the power of God's healing touch. Maybe he believed listening to the channel would change her prognosis. Maybe he needed it more than she did. Regardless, I always resented him for that show of selfishness.

Suddenly, I wasn't so confused or unsure. I pushed the door all the way open and walked into the room. I think something in me wanted to see him. I needed to remind myself of the person that turned his back on me so I could be sure I was prepared to walk away from him.

The room was like any other hospital room I'd seen over the years. Bland gray-green paint covered all four walls. a dimly lit bathroom sat awkwardly in the corner. A cushioned chair rested between the bed and the bathroom. Opposite the door was a lone window overlooking the parking lot. From where I stood, I could see Zoe's car. On the wall opposite the television was a long shelf with a basket of medical supplies including gauze and anti-bacterial wipes.

He was connected to several machines that emitted a low humming sound throughout the room. The red and green lights on the monitors blinked and changed and told the best and worst of his lifetime. I took all of this in and remembered just how much I hate hospital rooms.

He looked up, startled, and then muted the television as a smile swept across his face. The expression wasn't returned. At least not by me. I assumed I looked pissed off. Actually, there was a small mirror on the opposite wall that confirmed my assumption.

His blue and white hospital gown hung off one shoulder. He appeared so small, so frail. I remembered my father being a stocky man. This man, older and smaller, was a different version. Several tubes stuck out from under his gown, and I reminded myself of the choice I'd made to walk inside.

"Well, look at who we have here!" He kept his smile despite the growing dissatisfaction on my face. Zoe moved around me and stepped closer to the bed as he continued talking. "I have prayed for this moment, and I am so glad God blessed me to see this day."

I didn't budge from where I was standing.

"Hey, Dad. Yvette and I wanted to see how you're doing." Zoe smiled at him and patted his hand. She glanced back at me and noticed my expression.

He followed my gaze as I looked at the monitors. There were so many colors and lines and words on the screens all saying the same thing. This man's ill, and no matter what the doctors do, he will probably die. There was an internal tug of war on my heart. Seeing him so small and weak saddened me.

"Yvette, you can come closer. I ain't gone bite." His statement was supposed to carry the levity of a joke, but I didn't move or smile.

"Dad, how are you feeling?" Zoe's tone was one of sincerity and concern.

"I'm doing okay, baby girl. The doctors say this cancer is trying to get the best of me. But they don't know what I know." He paused for dramatic effect.

"I know in John 1:1 it says, 'In the beginning was the word and the word was with God and the word was God.' God decides what happens next and only *His* will matters. Until He dims my light, I'll keep on kicking and shining."

He motioned to the cushioned chair and a tan folding chair on the other side of the bed. "Grab some chairs and sit down, girls. Spend some time with your old man."

Zoe pulled the cushioned chair closer to the bed, sat down, and took his hand into hers again. I still didn't budge. It wasn't because I didn't want to sit down. But, if I sat down, I'd be committing to moving forward. I'd be accepting him back into my life, and I wasn't prepared for that just yet.

He chatted with Zoe, giving a status update on his condition and confirming what Aunt Sandy had already told me. I closed my eyes and inhaled then exhaled deeply. I tried to bring forth everything I'd learned during a recent meditation retreat. I needed to slow my mind and my heartbeat. When I opened my eyes, I found Zoe and my father looking at me.

"Uh, listen, girls. I know I ain't do right by y'all back then, and I've been waiting for the chance to tell you what's on my heart. I'm sorry for hurting you. I'm sorry for not being there for you. I'm sorry for you having to lose two parents because I wasn't strong enough to be the father you needed. But you know I never stopped loving either of you."

Tears streamed down his cheeks as he spoke.

"Yvette, you have a little girl so you know parenting don't come with no map. And I'm not making excuses, but I need y'all to understand. I loved your mother with everything in me. I went through a deep depression when she died. I couldn't sleep. I couldn't eat. I couldn't preach. I felt betrayed by God and rejected by everybody else. I didn't just lose my wife, I was losing myself. I know you girls needed me, but I ain't think I could be of use to no one back then. Your mother was my first love and soul mate and as long as I live, my heart will have a place for her."

Zoe looked down at him and said without pause that she forgave him. I sensed her sincerity from across the room. As they embraced, years of betrayal were forgotten and forgiven. He accepted her forgiveness just as she'd accepted his apology. A tear rolled down my cheek and I wondered why my feet were still so solidly planted by the door. I'd become an outsider wrongly bearing witness to such a loving moment between a father and his daughter.

"I had to find a way to move on. My life and my health depended on it. I'm not talking about Mary or the house or anything material. I'm talking about my sanity and my faith. They were in jeopardy, and I had to do my own soul searching."

My father asked Zoe to hand him the small, wooden box sitting on a side table beside the bed. Somehow I missed it when I first walked in the room. I watched as she tried to gently place the brown and black box into his hands without getting entangled in the wires running into and out of his body. I saw his hands, much older and recognizably weak, but still in need of a manicure.

The waves of dark brown wood along the black box's edge contrasted well against the lightness of the sheets. He turned it to face him, and the overhead light caught the shine from a gold-plated square that was welded to the back wall. I saw something engraved on the square, but I was too far away to read the words. He pulled back the top of the small jewelry box to reveal a gold watch and two rings. I knew instantly that one was my mother's wedding ring. I'd always admired it. The gold, etched band glistened under the light while eight small, diamonds formed comfortably into a marquis shape.

The second ring was also yellow gold with intricate details of curves and lines that all came together to compliment three middle stones. Resting in the center was a round emerald, representing Zoe's birth month of May. On the opposite ends were round stones of pink tourmaline. We were born in different generations and circumstances, but only four days separated me and my mother from birth. The rings remind me of the years we shared and the assumed plans for a future that never presented itself.

"Yvette, I think your mother would want you to have this," he said while extending the wedding ring in my direction.

My eyes darted between him and the ring in his outstretched hand. Here was something that had been a symbol of their love and commitment, built on a common and shared promise. I struggled because I knew he was trying to move us beyond that hot August day. He wanted to right his wrongs, but this moment reminded me of all the wrong choices he'd made. It was every time he'd posted a happy birthday on social media to Mary but never a said a word of remembrance about my mother on any day. It was him choosing to be a father to someone else that didn't share his last name. It was how cavalierly he seemed to want to rid himself of reminders of his past with us while clinging to his life with Mary and Vera. I crumbled.

I should have run to his bedside and given him the hug he wanted or the forgiveness he needed. I should have told him how much I missed him being part of my life and how much I desperately yearned to have him back in it. I should have taken care of him like I did my mother when she was dealing with the possibility of her death. In that instant I felt all those things but even more, I felt like walking away. So, I did.

I can't say for sure what made me leave. But I gave him one last look as tears fell from my eyes and walked away. For my father, that was our last father-daughter memory. It hurt him just as that August day sixteen years ago had hurt me. I didn't remind him of the definition of unconditional love. I didn't need to tell him how many other choices he had besides pushing us aside. I didn't have to give an impassioned speech on how much he'd failed me. Because in the end, as he heard my footsteps get farther and farther away, he already knew.

CHAPTER 15

YVETTE

As my hand pushed the lever on the main hospital door, I exhaled for the first time in what felt like ten minutes. I understood exactly how that little boy felt when he got outside.

My chest rose and fell as I took deep breaths. My lungs responded as though the air inside had been tempting but unreal. Or maybe I'd been holding my breath the entire time. I tried to process what had just happened. I saw my father. He spoke to me. I looked at him. I left.

I paced back and forth in the parking lot near the main entrance, waiting on Zoe to follow behind. After a few minutes, I realized my leaving would have little bearing on her timing. She came to make amends, and my erratic behavior wouldn't spoil her plans. Feelings, known and foreign, washed over me. I kept replaying the last few minutes in my mind. From the stale hospital smell to the look in his eyes before I walked away, I reflected on it all. What did I just do? Why didn't I ask him the questions I've kept bottled up inside for years? Why couldn't I forgive him? I pondered question after question until I was exhausted.

After taking a seat on a nearby bench, I pulled out my phone.

"I saw him," I said when I heard a familiar hello on the line's opposite end. Christopher started to say something, but I cut him off. "I just couldn't say anything to him. It's like we were back at the house all those years ago, and I felt dismissed and rejected all over again."

He listened quietly as I again poured out every detail from signing in to my current status on the bench.

"Okay, well do you want to go back inside?" The question gave me pause because I never considered that to be an option.

"No, I think it's best I don't."

Christopher tried to convince me to go back in at least to say a few words, but I wasn't listening. It had taken a lot for me to go to his room the first time, and I was disappointed with the outcome. The experience showed me that no apology could erase a lifetime of hurt, and there was no need to work through things now. Over the years, I'd given too much energy toward hating him, so finding love and forgiveness now was only an illusion.

Christopher and I talked for a few more minutes. I wanted to speak to Kayla, but she was at a play date with one of her friends. I needed to hear my daughter's voice and remember what it felt like to be a parent: to have demands on your time and resources and emotions. I needed a way to understand how he could leave us the way he did. How he could dispose of our love and affection with the shrug of a shoulder.

After hanging up with Christopher, the phone vibrated in my hand, and Sandy's face was on my screen.

"Hey, Aunt Sandy." In some ways, talking to her felt like talking to my father. Given I couldn't find anything to say to him, I hoped to avoid talking to her.

"Vet, how are you? I've been thinking about you." She sounded concerned and without judgment.

"I'm doing okay, auntie. It's been a long couple of days." I sighed into the phone.

"I can imagine. I know this isn't how you planned on spending your vacation."

"Nope, but I guess it's like that old adage about life happening while we're making plans."

We both chuckled softly, recognizing the tension flowing through the invisible phone line.

"Have you gone to the hospital yet?"

"Actually, I'm outside sitting on one of the hospital benches right now. I came with Zoe."

My aunt didn't say anything for a few seconds, I guess she thought I'd provide details so she wouldn't have to ask.

"I went inside, he apologized, and I left."

"Did you actually talk to him?" Aunt Sandy knew how to read between the proverbial lines.

"Um, well kinda. He talked and I listed but…umm…well…no I didn't."

She was a bit agitated by my response but didn't dare tell me so. Instead, she spoke with a sheer exterior of disappointment. Each sentence stinging more than the last.

"Yvette, I know you believe you have this thing figured out. But if I may, I'd like to share a bit of wisdom with you."

I thought back to that night so long ago when she shared a past of which I'd always been unaware. Sharing her truth and wisdom about Oliver had resulted in me being happily married. She had been right back then so maybe she'll be right now. I encouraged my aunt to continue speaking even though she didn't need my agreement.

"There was a time when I was angry with your father, too. He's my brother, and I'll always love him, but I didn't like how things happened with you girls or with that house. As easy as it was to be upset and give him the cold shoulder, it was better for us to talk about how we each saw things. He heard what I had to say, and we could either agree or agree to disagree. Regardless of what happened in your twenties, you can't keep holding him hostage for you not having your mother around. You say this is about him abandoning you, but I believe you blame him for losing her. That was God's call, not his, and you can't make him the focus of that anger."

I was stunned by my aunt's words. I didn't blame my dad for losing my mom. I blamed the brain tumor that came from the metastasized cancer. How could I hold him responsible for that? I didn't. I don't. At least, I never considered that a part of my anger. Aunt Sandy was a smart woman, rarely wrong. I sank deeper onto the bench as my mental reel clicked through all the feelings and internal battles I'd had since I was twenty-four years old and motherless. I didn't believe it was a case of blaming him for losing her. Rather, I created an expectation of him given I had lost her. I expected him to be the type of man his congregation saw him to be. I wanted him to be the man that had made a promise to me…to us. I expressed this to my aunt.

"Vet, don't you think he was hurting? I know the years have been hard for him because he loves you girls. Right now, you're being unfair. You expected him to act in a way you decided made sense in your mind and then continue to fault him for not playing the part that you alone scripted. That'll always set you up for disappointment."

"I get he was hurt and sad. I'm not blaming him for being human. I'm not even upset with him for remarrying and choosing to move on beyond his grief. But how did that result in him forgetting he already had two kids? At some point, he should've reached out to us. He should've taken the first step."

"He needed time to be sad and hurt and selfish just as you and Zoe. He never forgot he had you girls. But by the time the dark cloud had lifted, you'd already pushed him outta your life."

Heat rose in my chest, and I couldn't distinguish guilt from anger. How dare everyone continue to make me the bad guy? He was the bad guy. He was the failed parent, and I was the scorned child.

"Was it my fault he didn't visit me in the hospital when I had fibroid surgery? What about when he didn't attend my wedding or send any form of congratulations. When was the last time I received a birthday card from him? Was I the one that didn't try to get to know my granddaughter for the past twelve years? I live in Philadelphia, and he's never once been to visit us. I know he's been on planes because they've been to the Bahamas. But I guess planes don't fly north or am I still being unfair?"

As my emotions rose, I couldn't remain seated. I stood beside the bench, trying not to yell into the phone. There's a difference between taking a year or two off to clear your head but he chose to get remarried, parent someone else's child, and disregard his own kids. Even if I held him to a high standard, he could've at least tried. Instead, he chose to exit the whole damn situation. How dare Sandy or anyone else challenge me on fairness. I was beyond pissed off.

"I understand that Vet but what does that past have to do with today? Okay, he didn't send you birthday cards or call but you told him to never contact you. Even when he did, you didn't respond. So you're upset because he didn't force himself into a life that you fought for years to lock him out of?"

"Yes! Exactly! He should've fought harder! He owed it to us not to give up so easily." I yelled as tears covered my face.

I fell back onto the bench as indignation, sorrow, and contrition overcame me.

"Aunt Sandy, I apologize for yelling."

"I know niece, I know."

My guilt doubled as I heard the hurt in my aunt's voice. It was the first time Sandy's voice matched her age.

She gave no resistance as I respectfully ended the conversation. I loved my aunt, but this is why in sixteen years, we dared not discuss my dad.

Chapter 16

VERA

The garage door closed with a loud thud which woke me from a peaceful sleep. I looked over at the alarm clock and realized Aunt Sandy would be here to pick me up in less than an hour. I rolled over onto my stomach and stared at the acoustic ceiling. Thousands of little paint specs stared back at me. Faint sounds were coming from the kitchen. Mom was probably making a fresh pot of coffee. She's usually only thirty minutes behind dad in leaving the house.

I kicked my legs over the side of the bed and willed myself to get moving. My drawers were overflowing with clothes, but I couldn't find anything to wear. I looked in the closet and spotted a pink and white knit dress. I didn't remember if Aunt Sandy and I were running errands, working in her garden, or doing something equally boring. It wasn't that I didn't like spending time with my aunt but summer break went by so quickly. I'd be a senior next year so this was the last summer when my friends and I could hang out and have fun before separating and going off to college. Every now and then Aunt Sandy would let me go over to

Veronica's house for one of her impromptu pool parties but not as much as I'd like. I pulled a dress from the hanger and threw it on the bed.

I showered, dressed, and stepped into the kitchen just as the garage door closed again. *Have a great day to you too mom.* I grabbed a banana, a bottle of water, and my shoulder bag before heading outside. I liked to wait outside on the shaded porch and watch people as they headed off to work. It's also nice because morning and late afternoon were the only times when the Georgia sun wasn't unbearably hot. I took a seat on the porch and waited for my aunt. Across the street, Mr. Johnson barely missed his trashcan as he backed out of his driveway. The man is almost eighty years old. It's probably time he had his license revoked. I smiled and waved as he passed by.

His near accident reminded me to pull our trashcan around to the front. I forgot last week, and mom wouldn't let me hear the end of it. Fortunately, I was done with my banana so I added it to the waste. As I walked to the end of the driveway, pulling the plastic bin behind me, I noticed the little red flag was upturned on our mailbox. I headed over assuming it was a mistake. But when I peered inside and saw a small envelope nestled in the large tube, I was intrigued. I removed it and was surprised to see a Philadelphia address. I slid my fingers over Yvette's name. Why was dad sending her a letter? I didn't recall hearing anything about Yvette over the dinner table. Was he trying to keep this a secret? I wondered if mom knew. I dug the heel of my sandal into the grass around the mailbox post and wondered if this letter would change anything or would it change everything.

Questions clouded my mind as I stood frozen in front of

our mailbox. The letter was light, innocent even, in my hands. I looked at Yvette's name again and wondered what he'd said. She'd been so mean and selfish to my father for the past two years. The only thing she cared about was that house and after he gave it to her, she didn't want anything else to do with him. She was so cold and distant and never made an effort with me or my mother. Now he's writing her a letter.

Heat rose in my chest. Before thinking about it, I closed the lid on the mailbox, pulled down the flag, and stormed over to the porch where my shoulder bag sat. I quickly stuffed the letter inside and immediately felt guilty. Wasn't it a federal crime to take someone's mail? What if he wasn't apologizing but instead asking her to stay out of our lives forever. I kept thinking of new reasons for the letter, but they all pointed back to the possibility of me losing the one father I'd come to love. I couldn't compete with his biological daughters. It wasn't merely that they're beautiful and smart, it's that they already have a shared past with him of which I was never a part.

I looked in my bag at the crumbled envelope and considered putting it back into the mailbox. It'd be wrong to keep it from my stepsister and jeopardize my stepfather's trust. I repeated those words as I descended the steps of the porch and walked down the driveway. Each step sounded more resolute than the one before it. When I was a few feet from the mailbox, Aunt Sandy pulled onto our street and stopped in front of the house. I took my hand from inside the bag and jumped into her car with the fakest smile I could muster.

I snapped awake, struggling to catch my breath and slow my heartbeat. With every second that passed, the memory from so long ago faded from my thoughts. Beads of sweat lined my forehead and the collar of my pajama top. I quietly left the bedroom and headed for the kitchen. Fortunately, Damien was a heavy sleeper and didn't budge.

I was seventeen when I found that letter. I was young, confused, and… wrong. I hated to admit it, but I was wrong for not putting it back in the mailbox. I sensed it then and I was sure of it now. For years I'd justified it as an act of protection. I was keeping my family safe. I was shielding my father from more heartache at the hands of his insensitive daughters. But after knowing how much my action had cost him, I had to accept the truth. I'd broken something a decade couldn't repair—his heart. He'd been hurt and alone. Maybe that letter was a way for him to repair what he'd damaged, and I denied him that right.

Before I could change my mind, I grabbed a sweat suit from my bedroom, a pair of running shoes, and my car keys. I left a note for Damien on the nightstand. Hopefully, he'd see it and not be worried. I backed my Volkswagen EOS out of the garage and hoped the loud thud from the garage door didn't wake my husband and daughter. I pushed on the accelerator and hoped no cops were on the road. I needed to talk to my father.

The hospital was busier than I'd assumed for the middle of the night. I guess injury and sickness don't rely on clocks. I checked in at the front desk then followed the short hallway to his room. Usually, visitors were only allowed during certain hours but due to his prognosis, the nurses rarely enforced the rule. I slowly pushed open the door and peeked my head inside. He was lying in the fetal position facing away from me. I quietly stepped inside the room, leaving the door slightly cracked behind me.

The light blue blanket was tightly tucked under the sides of the mattress. His body looked smaller than it had only a few days before. I tiptoed over to the empty chair beside the bed and sat facing his back. I heard faint snores coming from the opposite side. My eyes watered as I considered all the things I should've told him but never did. How many more chances would I have to tell him how blessed I'd felt to have him as a father? How many days would go by with me keeping a secret that could've changed his life? A series of beeps disrupted my thoughts. I looked behind me to see several words and numbers in bright green and red flashing on the large monitor.

I turned back toward my father and the floodgates opened. I tried to cover my mouth so I wouldn't wake him. I lowered my head onto the side of the rail and wept. After a few minutes, I heard him shift in the bed. His frail hand found its way to the top of my head.

"Vera, what's wrong? What you doing here so late?"

He was more concerned about my well-being than his own. After adjusting the bed to an upright position, he put on his glasses. I tried to look at him but couldn't. He continued patting the back of my head and before I knew it, I'd stood and was leaning over the bed, sobbing into his chest.

"C'mon now, what's going on? What's this about?"

With every moment of silence that passed by, his level of concern increased. He gently pushed me back to look into my eyes. I stood there feeling sad and vulnerable, ashamed even. He lowered his chin and stared at me over the top of his eyeglasses.

"Ain't no need to feel guilty for being a child. You did what you thought you needed to do to protect yourself. I understood it then and I understand it now. I loved you then and I love you even more now."

I lifted my eyes and looked at my father. He nodded slowly and then pulled me back into him.

"And just in case you're wonderin', I forgive you."

He wrapped his arms tightly around my shoulders as I wept. I wanted to ask how long he'd known. How he'd found out? But in that moment, none of those questions or answers mattered.

CHAPTER 17

YVETTE

For the next two days, I watched Zoe go back and forth to the hospital. We didn't discuss where she was going and what she was doing because the silence spoke well enough for both of us. Christopher continued to offer support from a distance, but I could sense a growing tension. Given what had happened the last time he disagreed with my feelings, he was choosing to refrain from offering more than a few words of support.

The ride home from the hospital was a long and awkward one for Zoe and me. I'd disappointed her. By not allowing our father the benefit of forgiveness, I'd stolen my sister's fairytale ending.

On the third day, she finally broke her silence and sat beside me on the loveseat. I closed the cover on one of my favorite books and looked at her. Santiago and his journey for treasure would have to wait.

"Yvette, you talk a lot about consideration and fairness, but I've watched you throw both of those concepts out the window when it comes to him."

"How do you mean?" I asked taken aback.

"Well, you haven't once thought about this situation from his point of view. You've been so busy thinking only of your feelings, you haven't been open to anything else. This man is dying, and you think the considerate thing to do is make him work overtime for your forgiveness or to discard him like he doesn't matter?"

I looked at Zoe with a mixture of sadness and frustration. How could I discard someone who pushed me away?

Before I could say anything, Zoe patted my knee and shook her head while starting to stand.

"I'm going to the hospital. Let me know when you're ready to grow up."

"What happened with Jared?" The question was unexpected and unwelcomed. She slowly turned to look at me, and I felt horrible for even mentioning his name. A deep sadness overcame her. It was a look I hadn't seen since we were much younger. She exhaled deeply and sat back down on the opposite end of the loveseat, leaving more space than necessary between us.

"Things became too…complicated," she said while looking off into the distance. "Jared was a great guy, and I love him to this day. He just wasn't the right guy for me." She finally looked in my direction, and I saw in her eyes how much those words misaligned with her heart. She became comfortable pushing people away, and Jared had been no different.

"Complicated? I thought you both loved one another and wanted to be together. What happened to change that?" I tried not to pry, but I wanted my sister to see how easy it is to accuse someone of being unforgiving and inconsiderate rather than being introspective and recognizing her own shortcomings. She discarded Jared because he didn't fit into her mold, and now she sat there judging me for doing the same thing.

"Yvette, at this point it doesn't really matter. Things changed, and that's the end of the story."

With that, she got up and walked out of the room and out the door.

I sat in silence for about ten minutes before deciding to get some fresh air. I grabbed a sweater and headed outside. The street was fairly quiet, as most of the small children that once gave it life had left home and planted roots in other cities and states. The neighborhood was now filled with older couples, beautiful gardens, and the occasional dog.

As I came around the house from the garage, I glanced toward the steps where I'd waited that August day. They looked smaller now. If my father had given his little speech that day, I would've listened. I would've showered him with forgiveness. But on that day, my feelings didn't matter. My love wasn't good enough, and my forgiveness was not his desire.

Sounds of birds chirping filled the clear blue sky. I walked toward the end of the driveway and hesitated before stepping out into the street. My feet casually walked, and I followed. When I got to the end of the road, I turned left since I rarely went in that direction. I wanted to see and feel something different. As I approached the first side street, I caught a glimpse of an older couple, maybe in their early sixties, climbing out of a black 2011 Chrysler. I heard low laughter as they teased one another about parking the car too close to the garage wall. I stopped and watched their interaction. The man escorted his wife around the car and to the door, smiling and regarding her with the utmost care.

Sadness washed over me. My parents were supposed to be that couple. My mother should've been able to see sixty and experience having a love that spanned time.

I closed my eyes and pictured my parents sharing a laugh or a kiss. Theirs was a fluid motion, a rhythmic dance filled with purpose and passion. I remembered how beautiful my mom had looked in her flowing red dress and silver heels when they attended the city's Valentine's banquet. Her caramel skin glistened against the delicate pearls that adorned her ears and neck. Her hair, pinned in an up-do, left a few curls sweeping across the sides of her face. My father wore a gray suit with a white shirt and red tie, matching my mother's dress perfectly. They moved as one soul around the living room as my father hummed a song that only they knew. They posed for pictures, making sure to entertain us by acting both serious and goofy at times. Their love was palpable. They had reverted back to being those two teenagers that had met in a packed school hallway on an early winter's day. That's how deep their love flowed. It was an authentic and active love. It was one that everyone around them envied. Zoe and I were enamored by their union. It became the standard for the definition of love for our adolescent and adult selves.

I thought back to family vacations and how my mother always had matching outfits for us. One year during on a trip to Disney World in Orlando, we all wore white tops, denim shorts, and white shoes. We looked like the dorkiest family at the theme parks, but it made her happy, and we were happy to oblige. We smiled in pictures, never realizing the fashion wouldn't survive the test of time. But having the photos meant so much. Especially with her being gone.

I held the memories for as long as possible. I opened my

eyes, startled, to the sound of a door closing. Although my hands were sweaty and my mouth dry, my eyes were seconds from being filled with tears. Without thinking, I turned back toward the house.

I sat on the top front step. This visit was supposed to be about spending time with family in a peaceful and more slow-paced environment. For the past few days, my feelings had been all over the place. Everyday brought with it more stress, and peace was nowhere to be found. One of my professors once told me, "Peace happens only when you die. It is a carrot presented during life to make dying easier to accept." I always thought he was a bitter old man. I'd felt a lot of things since landing in Georgia, but peace was far from one of them. Maybe the surly old man had a point.

Not more than fifteen minutes went by before Zoe's car pulled into the driveway. Instead of parking in the garage, she stopped short. As soon as I saw her face, I knew what had happened. She ran to the steps, and I grabbed her into my body.

She sobbed loudly and without pause. I closed my eyes and felt the magnitude of her pain. I lifted my head toward the sun, feeling a flood of heat across my face. I wasn't sure what to do or say. I didn't add to Zoe's comments or reply to her rhetorical questions. I sat in silence as my little sister spilled her heart to me.

Our father had just died.

CHAPTER 18

YVETTE

My mother died on what for most people was an insignificant Thursday in May. For me, it was a Thursday three days before Mother's Day and four days before Zoe's twentieth birthday. On that Thursday, my mother and I both became forever linked with new statistics.

It had begun like any other day with us sleeping in the hospital waiting room and eating from the hospital cafeteria. Three close friends had flown in once we were told the inevitable was near, and they hadn't left my side. After breakfast, my father and two aunts watched television in my mother's room because for them, it also seemed an insignificant Thursday. Within thirty minutes, our lives would start down the path on which we were now. My father would tell us that our mom's breathing had become hollowed and less frequent. Zoe and I would rush to her bedside. From opposite ends we would each hold her hand and tell her how much we loved her. We would wonder if she could hear us because she'd been in a coma for two days and receiving heavy doses of morphine. Palliative care was the name doctors gave it.

Internally, we'd struggle to balance the truth of the scene with the boundless hope we'd come to consider. We would try to say all the things we never knew needed to be said until that very instant. I'd bend down, and as a tear fell from my cheek to hers, kiss my mother and whisper that it was okay. I'd tell her not to be worried about Zoe. That I'd take care of her. I promised to be stronger than the pain because I didn't want her to be in pain any longer. With all the adoration and gratitude within me, I gave my mother permission to let go. I allowed her the freedom to release her grasp on our world so she could find peace in another. With those words—or maybe it was just a coincidence of time—my mother's life came to an end.

When we arrived at the house less than an hour later, things felt different. My hands were shaking, and my tongue was numb. Sounds were muted, and I felt unsure that I'd ever be able to *feel* again. i went to my parents' room and lay on their bed. I glanced at my mother's neatly organized toiletries in the bathroom and missed her more than my heart thought possible. I desperately tried to inhale her perfume on the comforter or feel her presence within those four walls.

It had only been a short while, and I was already starting to feel traces of her drifting away. No one doubts the difficulty in losing a loved one, but I feared living a lifetime of losing her over and over again. If it happened in one place and time, it would be somewhat easier to accept. But what about days or months later when I wanted to remember a funny comment she made but couldn't quite recall details? A phone call was no longer an option after that very significant Thursday. The sound of her voice would become more of a whisper as the years passed. Photos would become the best way to make sure her features would be forever defined in my memory. Every memory and every detail that became more distant meant losing her all over again. But with guilt attached. Guilt because how could I forget my mother's voice or the warmth of her embrace? How could I not remember her recipes or favorite book or how to mimic her dance moves?

The tears started long before I noticed. Zoe joined me on the bed a few minutes later, and we both fell asleep as our collective tears stained the sheets.

At some point, our father arrived at the house along with my mother's things from the hospital. He'd stayed behind to complete paperwork and do whatever grieving families have to do when someone dies. He was a pastor, so he knew the process better than most. As he opened the bedroom door and entered, I could hear several voices in the kitchen and throughout the house. He looked at me briefly, and I saw the face of a man that had fought for his soul's mate and lost. He put the items in the closet and then went over to close the bedroom door. He came and sat on the edge of the bed and held out his arms. Zoe and I fell into his embrace, and the three of us sat drained and defeated. It had been a hard journey, and even though it was over, it was only the beginning. The end of my mother's pain equated to the sobering start of ours.

"I love you girls so much," he repeatedly whispered.

He promised to take care of us and reminded us of the need to be strong for our mother and her memory.

"Your mother raised you to be smart and capable young ladies. She was so proud of both of you, and so am I."

He told us to never forget we'd always be a family.

"I'm your father, and no matter what, I'll always be there for you. Nothing and no one can come between us. Do you girls hear me? I promise not to ever let anything come between us."

CHAPTER 19

YVETTE

Christopher and Kayla arrived the day after my father died. The funeral would be held in four days, on a Saturday. I considered asking Christopher to leave Kayla in Philadelphia with his mom but decided against it. Zoe was taking the news so hard. I figured seeing Kayla was one of the few things that could possibly lift her spirits.

I was overwhelmed with emotion when my husband and daughter pulled into the driveway. Even though it had only been a few days, I missed them terribly. Christopher and I talked every night, and it was clear he felt pulled in opposing directions. While he wanted to give me some space, he also felt obligated to ensure I wouldn't do something irreparable. He needed me to return to Philadelphia as a whole wife and mother, not a fragile and broken little girl.

As soon as her feet hit the pavement, I took Kayla into my arms and squeezed her small frame into mine. Seeing the two of them reminded me of a life that existed miles away. In another place and time, I am strong and stable. I make logical decisions and am not led by wavering emotion. The past few days made that reality seem more distant. It had surely not been that place or that time.

Kayla monopolized Zoe's attention as soon as she was released from my grasp. She started talking and telling Zoe how much she couldn't wait to see her. Zoe swept her up into a playful hug as they both giggled like old friends. I loved watching the two of them together, and was grateful something was able to distract Zoe, even if it was only for a few minutes. Christopher came to stand in front of me, and I fell into his arms. His embrace was strong and steady. I closed my eyes and inhaled my husband's essence while he kissed my forehead and told me how much he loved me.

Zoe took Kayla into the house while Christopher and I headed toward the front steps. We didn't speak for some time, until he sat down and patted the cement, indicating for me to join him.

"So, how are you doing?"

He looked at me with eyes that knew my heart. I shrugged while taking a seat. I leaned into his body as he placed his arm around my shoulders. His orange cashmere sweater was soothing against my skin, and I vowed to remain in that position until forever was no longer an option.

"I'm okay, relieved that you're here."

There were more parts to my answer, but the words didn't come, and I decided not to force them.

"Sweetheart, I'll always be here for you. If you want to spend more time down here with Zoe after the funeral, just let me know. This can't be easy for either of you. She can always come up to Philadelphia, too."

I smiled at my husband while thanking the universe for such an understanding and giving spouse. I know he thought I was more emotionally unstable than I would admit, but frankly, I didn't care. My thoughts and feelings were all over the place, and I needed something familiar, something constant.

"Have you, um, talked to…umm…your…his umm…Vera, since he died?" Christopher asked the question with caution.

I sat up slightly but refrained from looking directly at him.

"No, but Zoe probably talked to her yesterday on her way home from the hospital."

For the first time, I considered his other family. Ours were not the only relationships where merely remnants remained.

"Well, Kayla's down here, and I'm sure they want to get Annie's mind off this tragic situation. Maybe you can try to meet Vera to see how she's doing and also use that opportunity to introduce the girls."

I didn't reply instantly to Christopher's suggestion, primarily because I was terrified it was a good idea. I shrugged and told him I'd think about it. I wondered if calling Vera at this point was even beneficial. The kids lived seven hundred miles apart. What if she slammed the phone down and refused to talk to me? What if she told me nonstop stories about how great of a father he'd been to her? I pushed those thoughts out of my mind and allowed my body to relax against Christopher's.

"Maybe I'll give her a call," I said, and Christopher tightened his embrace. He didn't speak, but his grin revealed genuine satisfaction. To him, this was a step in the right direction.

"How'd Kayla do on her earth science test?"

"She got an A but pretend not to know. She wants to give you the good news herself."

"That's great! She can tell me about it while I fix dinner."

Over a meal of halibut, salad, and green beans, we heard endless stories from the thoughts and adventures of a twelve-year-old. Either Kayla was an abnormally humorous child, or we were all fighting not to let our minds be burdened by my father's death. We laughed and remained in good spirits through dessert and our "goodnights" and "sweet dreams."

The next day, Zoe spent most of her waking hours meeting with Mary, Vera, Sandy, and the funeral director. She was enthralled with the details of the service. They discussed the burial suit, casket, announcements, funeral service location, limos, and everything in between. I pretended not to notice much of it.

That night, I found Zoe going through photo albums looking for the perfect pictures for the obituary and funeral program. At first, I considered going to the bathroom and returning to bed. Instead, I took a seat beside her and looked at the pictures. It was strange seeing him with people I didn't know and had never met. He was there smiling with Mary as they traveled the world—Barcelona, Cape Town, Bahamas—sometimes just the two of them and sometimes with larger groups. We perused the pages, witnessing a house and a lifetime of which we were never a part. Zoe picked up a loose picture that said "father-daughter" on the back. As she flipped it over, my stomach knotted. The picture was of him walking Vera down the aisle at her wedding. The knot tightened.

Zoe placed the picture on the coffee table, and we both just stared at it. I could think of nothing to say that would soothe our hurt and anger at that iconic symbol of fatherhood being shared with Vera. My heart grew icicles as Zoe's became increasingly more fragile. I pulled my little sister into me again and closed my eyes as she softly cried. This time, I offered verbal support in a reassuring voice. We'd be okay because we had survived a heartbreak that shook our foundation years before. I reminded her she'd spent time with him at the hospital and did everything possible to make him comfortable before he died. She had been a great daughter.

I struggled to keep my feelings under control. This meant a lot to Zoe, and honestly, it meant something to me. She was twenty when we lost our mother, and back then she'd needed a parent. Now at thirty-six, it was less important to be parented, but it was just as important to be loved—and found worthy of love. For the past few days, Zoe sat at his bedside because they both needed one another. He needed forgiveness, and she needed acceptance. They were able to give the other something no one else could. I looked down at my sister and wondered how many relationships this had infected.

I walked Zoe to her room and helped her into bed. She curled up into the fetal position, and I drew the covers over her shoulders.

"He has a daughter."

She turned to face me, and I saw the tears streaming down her face. I assumed she was somehow relaying how she felt about the picture of our father and Vera, but she continued.

"I found out a few months after we got engaged that Jared had a daughter from a previous relationship. She's five years old and lives in California with her mother. I guess it not only hurt that he chose not to tell me about her, it bothered me that she wasn't an active part of his life. We grew up with someone in our house that loved us and made sure we were provided for daily. Dad taught me how to ride a bike and drive a car and so many other things. Seeing Jared lack accountability to his daughter or his past pushed me to have a different perspective on what happened with our father. He was accountable to us, and even though we wanted him to forget his emotions and focus on ours when mom died, we were grown women. It wasn't his burden, it was ours, and we couldn't force him to take that on his shoulders. Jared was a coward, and no matter how many times he tried to make a relationship appear from a once-a-month phone call or an annual visit with his daughter, I could already see he wasn't the kind of man I wanted in my life. He wasn't the type of father I'd want for my child. That's why I broke up with him."

I looked at Zoe and fully understood her feelings, as I'd said yes to Christopher for the exact same reason. I told her how much I loved her and quietly closed her bedroom door behind me. I returned to the living room and turned over the picture. Zoe had walked away because Jared's inconsistency made her love and cherish the man our father had been. I knew how much a man could love his child. I see how Christopher cared for Kayla. When I considered their bond, it reminded me of the one I once had with my father. There was a time when he could never be at fault in my eyes. Throughout my childhood, he'd been everything I needed him to be. Why was that not enough? Why did he decide to turn away from that life? Unlike Zoe, as I remembered my father's infallibility, I didn't raise the pedestal. Instead, looking at the album and seeing the life he'd lived in absence of us stirred resentment and hurt deep inside.

Anger rose from deep within, threatening to cause an implosion. I had to be positive for Zoe, but it was becoming more difficult. I checked on Kayla and found her sound asleep. Next, I woke Christopher because I needed to talk. I made two cups of tea as thoughts ran through my mind. He sat at the kitchen table waiting for me to say something, but I didn't know how to start. After putting the tea in front of him along with a jar of honey, I took a seat across the table. He reached out to take my hand.

"Babe, are you okay?"

It was a simple question, but it asked so much. I looked up at him and shook my head.

"I'm angry, Christopher. I'm angry my mother died. I'm angry at the past sixteen years and how we got to this point. I'm angry that dying was the reason for him reaching out to us. I'm angry we're left here to resolve his mistakes. I'm angry he was more of a father to someone that wasn't of his blood than he was to me. I'm angry I lost a father sixteen years ago and he didn't give a damn."

I said all of this hurriedly, yet softly so as not to wake everyone in the house. Christopher held my hand tightly while coming around the table.

"Sweetheart, I hear how you feel, and I know this is difficult, but you have to get past the anger. It's only going to prevent you from finding peace in all of this."

There was that word: peace. The only person who was guaranteed peace was the one that's causing unrest for the rest of us.

"Christopher, I can't go to his funeral."

My husband looked at me with hints of surprise and concern, but he sensed my resolve.

"I probably can't change your mind, but how about you to sleep on it?"

I got up, grabbed the picture from the living room, and placed it in front of him. He looked down and then back up at me without saying a word.

"Who walked me down the aisle at our wedding? Who thought it was important enough to be there and to take pride in giving me away?"

He looked back down at the picture and took a sip of his tea. He knew the decision was made.

CHAPTER 20

VERA

It seemed more cars arrived with each passing day. Various makes and models lined my parent's driveway and most of their street. While half of the guests were family and friends, the other half were ministers and deacons from around the state. They'd all worked with my father and wanted to pay their respects to his family.

I tried to stop by, help around the house, and leave before noon each day to avoid the crowd. I usually found something in the kitchen to busy myself so I didn't have to sit around and reminisce with strangers. My mother knew what I was doing and fortunately, didn't say anything.

I parked the car in an empty space near the mailbox and called Damien to come outside and help carry the grocery bags. Everyday people brought canned sodas, pound cake, potato chips, and fried chicken as if those were the universal food items for grieving families. After a couple of days of nothing but junk food, I decided enough was enough. I went to the local market and picked up some fruit, vegetables, water, and bags of salmon to bake, air fry, and broil. I bought the kids peach mango ice pops and a few household items so mom didn't have to worry about running out.

Damien grabbed several bags from the trunk leaving only one for me to carry. He asked for the eighth time that day how I was doing to which I replied in the same way I had since my father died, by smiling and squeezing his hand. I appreciated his show of support but I needed a little bit of space, even from him. I didn't know how I was doing. Some mornings I felt okay, like I had the strength to pull through. But by evening, I wanted to curl up in a ball and do nothing but sleep or most often, cry. Annie came in and I handed her an ice pop before she grabbed Damien's hand.

"C'mon daddy," she said, "I have a new book from Miss Rachel. Can we read it together?"

Damien looked at me and I gestured for him to go with Annie. I appreciated the time alone.

I finished putting everything away and was throwing the bags into the trashcan when I heard someone come up behind me. I turned around to find my mother standing a few feet away.

"You were such a chubby baby. You had these chubby cheeks and I couldn't get enough of rubbing them against my cheeks 'cause they were so soft and squishy," she said with a faraway look in her eyes.

"And believe it or not, there was a time when you didn't want to go anywhere without me. You wouldn't let me out of your sight and I didn't want to leave the house without you. You were my little princess. I remember when I took you to day care for the very first time. It was a sad sight! I sat in the car crying like I'd lost my best friend. I cried all day long until it was time for me to pick you up."

My mother sat down at the dining room table. Her eyes were glistening, and she smiled as she spoke. I stood frozen wondering what had prompted her walk down memory lane.

"Vera, I don't know exactly when and I never figured out why but somewhere along the way, we drifted apart. I thought maybe it was because you were becoming a teenager and I remember how much friction I had with my mom at that age. I dismissed what was happening right in front of my eyes because I assumed we'd work through it eventually. It just never happened."

"Mom—." She cut me off.

"Wait, let me finish."

She got up from her chair and came to stand in front of me.

"You've been a great daughter and I'm so lucky to be your mom. You're kind-hearted and smart. You've raised my amazing granddaughter and found a wonderful husband to share your life. I'm so proud of you my little princess."

She kissed me on the forehead and gave me a tight hug. I felt her cheek rub against mine. I became overwhelmed with emotion. I wrapped my arms around her.

"I love you, mom."

"I love you too, Vera. Always."

With that, my mother turned and left the kitchen. I grabbed an apple and went in search of Damien. There were several people to speak to or be comforted by throughout the house. It took at least ten minutes just to make my way to the back door. I looked through the glass and saw Damien and Annie sitting on the porch swing reading her new book. They made faces and laughed as they turned the pages. Damien looked up and saw me in the doorway. I smiled at him so he wouldn't assume something was wrong. I looked at my daughter and thought about my mother's words. I hadn't known how to comfort mom after my dad's death so in some ways I'd kept my distance. I figured I'd follow her lead and assumed if she needed me, she'd let me know. I didn't know how much but I'd needed that hug and those words from her. I needed to know she was proud of me.

Guilt washed over me, and my smile faded. I put my hand on my stomach wondering how I might undo the mistakes of my past. I allowed fear to prevent me from confessing to my sisters and now our father was gone. Maybe if they'd known about the letter, they would've been able to reconcile sooner. I closed my eyes and when I opened them, Damien was standing in front of me. I pushed open the back door and stepped outside.

"You good?"

"Not really and I don't know if I'll be 100% good for a long time, babe. But there's something I have to do if I ever want to be okay again."

I kissed his cheek, noticing the puzzled expression on his face, and then went back into the house to find my cell phone. I sent Zoe a text asking for Yvette's number. There was no way I could go another day knowing I'd sabotaged their relationship with our father and they not know the truth. It'd be their decision to accept me or hate me but at least there'd be no more secrets. Seeing Annie with Damien crystallized what I'd done so many years ago. My daughter idolized her dad. Her face lit up every time he entered a room. Damien was her hero and my selfish actions had prevented two women from being able to have their hero in their lives. I may not have been the catalyst for their broken relationship, but my actions had caused a series of events and assumptions that led to its tragic end. My phone vibrated. I looked down at the ten digits staring back at me. It was finally time to tell the truth.

CHAPTER 21

YVETTE

The next morning, Zoe wasn't as understanding of my decision to skip the funeral. She called Sandy, and within an hour, they were both standing in front of me trying to change my mind. Based on their words, I was every form of selfish and insensitive. Regardless of what I said, they believed it was no excuse for missing the service.

"I'm not attending the service just because it's expected," I said with certainty.

"Yvette, you are so damn stubborn!" Zoe hurled another insult.

"Zoe, I'm not trying to hurt you, but we obviously feel very differently about this."

I was quickly growing irritated.

"Yvette, you realize this is the last time you'll be able to see your father. It's your chance to say goodbye and find peace."

"I'm so sick of people trying to comfort me by offering peace. Can you guarantee me peace, auntie? Can you promise me I won't feel sadness or hurt or disappointment anymore? No, you can't. So please stop trying to offer something you don't have the power to give."

I was done with feeling compelled to offer justifications for my feelings. I could hear Christopher's footsteps coming toward us. He slowly peeked around the corner and into the bedroom. Aunt Sandy turned to see him, and her face lit up.

"Christopher, it's so good to see you!"

She'd always been a big fan of his, and he was a fan of hers. They were similar in many ways, and I knew she reminded him of his deceased grandmother.

As they embraced, Sandy asked him to talk some sense into me. I rolled my eyes and sat on the edge of the bed. I recognized the black and brown jewelry box sitting on the armoire.

"Yvette knows how she feels, and while I may not understand, I have to respect her feelings. You guys should do the same."

His comment made me love him even more. I needed someone to at least respect my boundaries, and he was doing just that. He winked at me and we both smiled.

"Christopher has to say that because he's her husband, but he knows she's wrong. She's completely absorbed in her own feelings right now and isn't thinking about anything or anyone else." Zoe continued to voice her opinion, and at some point, I stopped listening.

"Zoe, who does it hurt if I don't go? Him? He's dead, so it's not as if he knows."

I looked at Christopher and the pair of freshly pressed black pants he was holding. He noticed my look of confusion.

"I know you've decided not to attend the service tomorrow, but if it's okay with you, I'd like to go and take Kayla."

My heart fell as I recalled only seconds believing we had the strongest partnership ever imagined. I walked over to the jewelry box.

"Why would you take Kayla? She doesn't need to see him or attend his funeral. She doesn't even know who he is."

Christopher came and stood beside me.

"Sandy sent us some pictures and I had her explain the situation to Kayla before we got here. Kayla wants to see him and say goodbye. I think we should let her."

I was completely floored.

"How could you do that behind my back?"

I looked back and forth between Christopher and Sandy, but both shrugged it off as if they'd done nothing wrong.

I left the room and went into the backyard for some fresh air. Everything was moving so quickly around me. Only a few days ago I was standing in a hospital room listening to my father ask for my forgiveness, and now I'm trying to defend not going to his funeral.

I'm so sorry for hurting you and not being there for you in the way that you needed. I never stopped loving either of you. His words echoed in my head. *I'm asking for your understanding.* His words had found their way into my dreams. He requested the impossible—my understanding. How could I understand him making us feel uncared for and unloved for almost two decades? How could I give him something that even I didn't understand? There were so many times when he could've made things right between us, yet that wasn't the path he chose. It's amazing the impact of one person's words and actions on another. How three simple words like I am sorry or I love you, when communicated in the right moment, can change a person's life. Unfortunately, when they aren't spoken at all, they can still do the same.

I couldn't oppose Kayla and Christopher attending the funeral. I owned my feelings and my decision not to attend, and I had to respect Christopher for doing the same. Plus, this would give Kayla an opportunity to meet Annie.

I went inside to get the car keys from Christopher. I had to spend some time alone with my thoughts. As soon as I walked in, I saw Kayla sitting on the sofa reading a book. She smiled up at me as I took a seat next to her.

"Sweetheart, I need to talk to you about something," I said softly while stroking her hair.

"Yes, mom?" Kayla had a way of making my heart melt without even trying.

I glanced at the words filling the pages of her book and silently wished she'd known her grandmother.

"I know your dad and Aunt Sandy talked to you about your grandfather already, but I want to make sure you don't have any questions or things you'd like to discuss with me."

I didn't want her to feel obligated to talk, but I wanted her to know I was there to talk or listen and be completely honest with her. She sat in silence for a few seconds as if trying to decide if she had any outstanding questions.

"Well, I do have one question."

I braced myself.

"Why didn't I meet my grandfather while he was still alive? I mean, didn't he want to meet me?"

Her innocence touched my heart. Seeing my daughter in that moment made it clear how my issues had trickled down and unintentionally affected her. My years of stubbornness had caused her feelings of insecurity.

I thought of my conversation with Sandy just days before and felt a pang of guilt. I shared fault for him not having been in Kayla's life or mine. I considered the special bond that my father was able to develop with Annie, a bond my daughter would never know.

"Kayla, your grandfather and I hadn't spoken in years, long before you were ever born. It all started shortly after my mother, your grandmother, died. His absence in your life had nothing to do with you so don't ever think that."

I paused.

"Honestly, you never met my dad because I was upset with him. I was angry and I allowed that to override what was probably in everyone's best interests, including yours. I'm so sorry for not giving you the chance to meet him. I know it's a lot to ask right now, but I hope one day you can forgive me."

"Of course I forgive you mom."

"Thanks sweetheart. You know what? On Saturday you'll get to meet your cousin Annie. She lives here and is a few years younger than you, but it'll be good for you two to get to know one another."

I took my daughter in my arms and held her for what felt like a lifetime. Deep down, I wished she had known her grandfather, too.

CHAPTER 22

YVETTE

I stood in the backyard looking at my phone as if it was a foreign object. *Make the call.* I tried to persuade myself to dial the numbers. It wasn't a novel concept. However, every time I got close to pressing a key, I panicked. *Make the damn call, Yvette.* I surprised myself with my forcefulness. The phone felt heavy in my hand as I pressed it against my ear.

"Hello?" I heard a familiar voice on the other end.

"Um…hi…Vera? It's Yvette. Is this an okay time?" I responded with apprehension.

"It's perfect. I was actually about to call you."

I detected surprise in her voice. Unsure of how to start the conversation, I did what's typical and second-guessed myself. What do you say to someone in this situation? Should I begin by telling her how sorry I am for her loss? That seemed more than a little strange considering the circumstance. So much had happened. The man that fathered us both, albeit in different ways and through very different seasons of our lives, had died.

"We haven't talked much over the past few years, but I wanted to see how you were doing as well as check on Annie."

Why was I brimming with unease? Vera and her mother took the only father I'd ever known, repositioned him in a new life, and didn't look back. I glanced up and saw Christopher staring at me through the patio door. After talking to Kayla, I'd told him I needed to make a phone call. He raised his eyebrows as if asking if everything was okay. I responded with a nod and thumbs up. He disappeared from the window.

"We're doing okay. Wow, Yvette. I must say this surprises me," she said while interrupting herself. "I mean, talk about interesting timing."

"Yeah, well I think it's time we cleared the air," I said while exhaling.

"I wholeheartedly agree."

Vera sounded nervous but I wasn't sure why. Although, she did say she was about to call me.

"You still sound so surprised."

"Well, you've spent all these years hating me, and now for you to call—it's just unexpected."

I tried to detect any sarcasm or bitterness in her voice but found none. She sounded genuinely surprised.

"Vera, I never hated you, and I don't hate you now. To be clear, I spent years hoping things would go differently, but they never did. He didn't fight for our situation to change. I didn't blame you. I blamed him."

My voice was relaxed and calm.

"If you only knew…" she trailed off.

"If only I knew what?"

"Yvette, your father loved you and bragged about you and Zoe nonstop. I grew up living in the shadows of two people I knew only through stories and photos. His very definition of 'daughter' was defined by the two of you. You don't think he wanted to have things go back to how they were before? He loved my mother, but as a married woman, I know how passion and intensity reveal themselves in words. That came out when he spoke of your mother. He appreciated my mom for being there when he was at his lowest, but he loved yours for being able to help him achieve his highest."

I listened to her words, trying to process them.

"Your father—our father—needed you to listen and understand. He patiently waited year after year for another chance. I waited, too. The first few years, I tried not to get too close to him for fear that you two would burst through the door and take him away. I tried to be everything you two had been, but I couldn't reach that golden stamp of approval. That's not to say he didn't love me, but I know it wasn't with the same mountain-moving love he had for you two. So, yes, it's surprising to have you on the other end of my line saying he didn't want things to change. You only say that because you don't have the privilege of the full picture."

Her words forced their way into my ears. I was taken aback by her forthrightness but also appreciative. It had always been easier for me to assume how he felt versus asking him directly. I spent years thinking *for* him because I refused to listen *to* him.

"Why are you telling me all this?"

Instead of diving into what Vera had just said, I decided to understand why she'd said any of it.

"Not until recently did I fully understand what happened and the key role I played in your pain. It's just…" her voice trailed off again.

"What? Just what?" I asked.

"Yvette, we should talk. Not over the phone but face to face. It's time you, me, and Zoe talked."

"Okay, why don't you come over Sunday night."

Confusion consumed me and I wondered what Vera wanted to discuss. Based on the current conversation, I expected another impassioned speech with an appeal to be closer as sisters or something.

"Actually, if you have time, we should talk today." I felt a lump in my throat. She was firm and clear. There was more behind her words than a speech or desire to be closer.

"Our family is hurting Yvette and we've all played a part. But we have daughters, and I'd rather they grow up as family and not strangers."

I heard the sincerity in her voice, and after my conversation with Kayla, I knew she was right. I was exhausted from fighting the ghosts of the past. My own daughter was suffering because of it—because of me. I was acting as selfishly as I'd always perceived my father to be and after sixteen long years, I finally saw it. I gave Vera the address and we ended the conversation. I walked into the house as her words replayed in my head.

He'd patiently waited year after year for another chance.

EPILOGUE

It was October 8, and I was officially forty-two. I don't quite know why I sat in the car wondering what to do next, considering I was settled in my decision—resolved in my actions.

I looked down at the flower arrangement sticking out of one end of the basket and smiled. It was time to do what I'd been waiting to do for years.

I put my hand on the handle and opened the door. My body moved with purpose. I stood outside the car and inhaled what felt like new air. Looking across the cemetery, I saw a field of loved, grieved, and sometimes forgotten people. Several of the graves were well-kept and had fresh flowers in sight. Others were almost overtaken by weeds. I said a quick prayer. For all the struggle and turmoil that's faced when one's eyes are open, it's sad to see this as the end.

As I walked toward a familiar spot, I remembered the adage about living life to the fullest and treating everyday as if it's your last or cherishing each minute and every moment and all of the sayings that are supposed to instill a sense in us that life is to be lived. The destination should always be an afterthought because the journey is the part where we can participate. That's the part we can actually influence. By the time we reach our final destination, it's simply a part of someone else's journey.

My feet stopped, and I looked to the left to find my

mother's smiling face. Her name was prominently displayed along with dates I remember every year regardless of how much I yearn to sometimes forget. I smiled at her picture and felt the first of many tears to hit my cheek. I truly missed her.

I opened the basket and removed half the carnations, setting them on her grave. Years ago, I realized how important it was for me to find a different way to celebrate her outside of visiting the cemetery. Living hundreds of miles away punctuated that need as I couldn't stop by whenever I wanted. At home, I lit candles, wrote notes, hung pictures, and everything else to preserve her memory. Being at her gravesite was different. Most likely because the visits have to be few and far between. It makes them unique—special.

I unfolded the paper in the front right pocket of my jeans and recited the words. Midway through, I realized I didn't need the paper because I knew the poem by heart. I continued spilling feelings of love and appreciation and genuine gratitude and commitment. These were the same stanzas I'd recited during the program at her church on our last Mother's Day together. I usually tried to find something material to give, but that year I was compelled to put the effort into giving her something from my heart. The universe clearly knew the following year she'd die three days before Mother's Day.

I finished the poem and wept for some time before refolding the paper and putting it back into my pocket. I apologized to my mother for not always being strong enough to do what she would've wanted. I smiled as she covered me in forgiveness.

During all of this, I didn't look to the right of her grave. But now, feeling even more certain of my decision, I turned to find my father's name and likeness. His smiling face looked at me from the small oval frame on the headstone. I returned his smile. Bouquets of flowers lined the granite wall, and a few balloons were tied to a vase filled with yellow roses. The color of the surrounding soil was darker than the other graves, hinting at a recent burial.

I removed the blanket from the basket and spread it between my mother and father. I placed the remaining carnations on my father's grave as I took a seat. Then, without hesitation or fear, I spoke. I said hellos and goodbyes that had been silenced for almost two decades. I told him about thoughts and feelings that spanned the entirety of our separation. I gave my father a glimpse into the life of which I'd selfishly locked him out. I told him about my career, my friends, and my family. I laughed when I replayed how I'd met Christopher and how we felt going through the birth of Kayla. I allowed tears to fall as I relived the emotions we struggled through during the miscarriage of our second child. I retrieved the photo album from the bottom of the basket and gave him a view into my husband and daughter, two people he'd never met. I sat and shared my life with my father under a setting sun.

Some people felt I was selfish and stubborn with how I handled things. At first, I disagreed. But now, I know my mistake. I saw my shortsightedness. I knew my father and I have fond memories of him. He was the man who held me in his arms after my mother died and vowed his commitment to his daughters and our mother's legacy. The person he became a few months later wasn't the man I wanted to remember. But in my mind, I would get to talk to the father I loved and missed only when this day came. As I told Vera, it's possible one letter could've altered everything, or it may not have altered anything. Too much of life had happened and changed us in a way that couldn't be undone. Our past sixteen years hinged on him not loving me on my terms. I needed to be valued and made a priority. I wanted him to love me in a way that clearly demonstrated how much he cared. Based on my conversation with Vera, he was practicing patience while I expected proactive persistence.

After I vented my frustration, I appealed to his spirit and asked for forgiveness. While I understood the pain and loneliness he felt when my mother died, my stubbornness allowed me to walk away in the hospital. I acknowledged how childish and misplaced my anger had been. It was clear I didn't allow him the same peace I'd always prayed for my mother. I was a product of their union. I reassured him of my love and gratitude. When I had no more words or pictures, I wept softly for the man that had given me life and somehow left it far too soon. With a sense of peace, I finally mourned the death of my father.

ACKNOWLEDGMENTS

Thank God for bestowing me with this story and blessing me with the opportunity to deliver it to you. This is a work of passion (and fiction!) many years in the making. Although it was conceived out of pain and brokenness, it was birthed as a symbol of hope and renewed faith in unconditional love. I sincerely thank everyone that inspired, encouraged, and supported me throughout the journey. It was your nudging that kept me from giving up and your show of confidence that wouldn't allow me to give in.

I thank my mother, ***Vanessa Yvette Bryant***, for continuing to inspire me even from the far reach of Heaven. You are greatly loved and missed.

To my sister, ***Brittany***, I will always love you beyond conditions. Remember to forever believe you are indeed powerful beyond measure.

To enduring friendships, ***Detreich and Troi***, thank you for valuing our bond beyond geography and time. You are the family I chose. Thanks for also choosing me.

To my father, ***Frankie Bryant***, thank you for your love.

To my grandparents, ***Annie Mary Ellison, Bennie White, and Ethelene Bryant***, looking down on me from above, thank you for helping create and define me.

To my ***Aunt Jackie***, thanks for not only being my mother's friend and confidante but being one of mine as well. Thanks for your feedback on the original manuscript.

To *Aunt Willie M. Johnson*, thanks for always offering a listening ear and reminding me of my talents.

To my aunts, *Mary Anne, Brenda, Linda, and Paula,* thanks for your loud cheers and silent prayers.

To *Mrs. Vera Holloway*, thanks for all the loving hugs you gave me not knowing how much I needed them. May you rest in love.

To *Yancey & Toby Grimes*, thanks for always making your home a safe and welcoming space for me.

To all my aunts & uncles—biological or not—thanks for helping me learn and grow in ways you couldn't imagine.

To my cousins and extended family, you guys keep me laughing. Thanks for busying my mind with game nights, jokes, dance-offs, holiday parties, vacations, and everything in between.

Thanks to *Kendra, Bianca, Nadja, Christina, Sonia, Janeen, and Brittany* for your feedback a decade ago with the original manuscript.

Marie Morrison, you did an amazing job on the original cover!

To my *B.R.C.S.* sisterhood, you ladies have inspired and reminded me to always think BIGGER. Your motivation pushes me to challenge my thinking and my writing.

To *Carolyn Sampson*, thank you for being an example of womanhood, elegance, and strength. I honor you.

To all friends, past and present that I didn't name but feel just as indebted to—thank you!

Mommy, I hope I continue to make you proud!

QUESTIONS FOR DISCUSSION

Q: Who was your favorite character in *Yesterday Mourning* and what did you most appreciate about him/her?

Q: In the Prologue, Yvette mentions the relationship with her father has become one filled with attorneys as intermediaries. Who do you believe had the primary responsibility of not allowing their relationship to become strained? Throughout the novel, did your perspective change?

Q: In referring to her mother's final days, Yvette believes that by she and Zoe being around, their mother was unable to "find peace in the end." Often, family and friends surround a person when they're nearing death. What impact, if any, has this novel had on your thinking about a person's final moments?

Q: Yvette never says a word to her father until the very end at his gravesite. After reading her explanation for why she chose not to speak to him, do you believe she was justified? Why or why not?

Q: While most of the main characters in *Yesterday Mourning* are named, the author chooses not to name the father. What could be her reason for this? What impact does it have on the story?

Q: Aunt Sandy tells Yvette a story about her three-year marriage to Oliver when Yvette questions accepting Christopher's proposal. How does the story of Oliver offer insight into Sandy's push for Yvette to mend the relationship with her father?

Q: What specific themes did the author emphasize throughout the story? What do you think she's trying to get across to the reader?

Q: Throughout *Yesterday Mourning*, the word "peace" is used by many of the characters. How do you define peace and do you believe Yvette's actions allowed her to find it in the end?

Q: Mary mentions having a strained relationship with Vera but towards the end, she tells her daughter she's proud of her and loves her. How do you envision their relationship now that the Pastor has died?

Q: What do you believe happens next for this family?

Q: Although the author includes a flashback of Vera hiding a letter from the Pastor to Yvette, the contents are never revealed. What do you believe the letter said?

A DISCUSSION WITH RENITA BRYANT

QUESTION: What inspired you to release an anniversary edition for *Yesterday Mourning*?

Well, so much has happened in the past decade! I've not only authored several other books, but I've published 200+ titles through Mynd Matters Publishing, the press I founded when I released the original version of *Yesterday Mourning*. My views have evolved on some matters and deepened on others. I know the pain of losing someone you love through death as well as the emotional struggle of losing someone that remains alive. I've learned how someone who loves you can also abandon you. I've learned the balance of letting go so you can grieve while also holding on in a way that allows you to honor a loved one and maintain some semblance of their presence in your life. It took years to understand exactly how that works. I wanted to bring back some of the themes because they are still relevant today. I've met thousands of people in the past decade through Mynd Matters as well as being involved in IBPA (Independent Book Publishers Association) and other entrepreneurial ventures and these topics still resonate. Forgiveness, grief, peace, love, parent-child trauma, abandonment—are all relevant and should continue to be explored.

When my mother lost her battle with cancer at the age of

forty-two, I was only twenty-four. I had just graduated from Florida A&M University's (FAMU) prestigious MBA program and started my career at a biotech in Philadelphia. Writing gave me the control I needed during a time in my life when I felt powerless. It helped me along my healing journey back then and even now as I re-read it for this new edition, it continues to heal and help me.

Being able to divulge all of my grief and confusion on paper was therapeutic. Writing *Yesterday Mourning* helped me come to terms with losing my mom and the role I've played in the existing dynamic with my dad.

QUESTION: Which was your favorite character to write, and why?

Without any doubt, I'd say the father. Having to understand him and write both ends of him—loving and absent, contrite yet unyielding—was interesting. Who he is at the beginning of the story is quite different than how he appears near the end and having to fold both of those into a short novel allowed me to think more deeply about my own parental relationships as well as my boundaries and thoughts on forgiveness.

QUESTION: Is there a message in your novel that you want readers to grasp?

I'd like readers to understand how two people can go through the same situation, endure devastating pain caused by that very event, and have two totally opposing perspectives coming out of it. Forgiveness is such a powerful notion and it often requires us to see someone else's truth.

QUESTION: Do you recall how your interest in writing originated?

My mother wanted to be a writer. I remember being very young and asking her about clouds and how they were made. Instead of giving me the scientific answer (which of course I later learned), she wrote a short story and then typed it and left it on my bed. She wrote an entire story for me. My mom made my passion for writing almost a given. I wish I still had that story because I would definitely publish it. One of my goals is to publish her work so she also has the (posthumous) title of published author.

QUESTION: What was the hardest part of writing your book?

Being so vulnerable—not simply during the actual writing but also after publishing it. As an author you struggle with the fear of releasing something you've grown a deep attachment to and not having others respect or appreciate it. I wondered if my friends and family would be able to understand *Yesterday Mourning* and if strangers would even buy it.

Now that it's been a decade since I released the first edition, I'm far less worried. So many people connected with the story and shared their thoughts with me. I know that while it's not for everyone, many people will resonate with the characters and feelings of grief, loss, forgiveness, resentment, and all the things that often keep us trapped within our own mental and emotional walls.

And if not, that's okay too. I'm at peace with either response.

QUESTION: Do you have anything specific that you want to say to your readers?

THANK YOU! I appreciate your time, feedback, and support. It humbles me when you say my novel moved you to tears or made you reconcile relationships that had been non-existent for years. I've attended book talks, both virtually and in person, and they've all made me feel so grateful. One group in Ohio had food and drinks all named after characters and locations in the book! It was so special and thoughtful (thanks Glory!).

QUESTION: What else have you published and what do you have in the pipeline?

For adult readers, I'm currently working on an extended poetry collection and a collection of essays about dating and relationships.

For young readers, I have two children's books currently available, *Rihanna's Can-Do Adventures* and *Santa's Holiday Mix-Up* (Holidayville Adventures). I've also released the companion coloring book *Santa's Holiday Mix-Up*.

Book 2 in the Holidayville Adventures series, *Holidayville's Lucky Easter Surprise*, will be released Spring 2025. *Roman's Fun Day at the Farm* will be released Summer 2025 and Book 3 in the Holidayville Adventures series, *Cupid's Most Thankful Thursday*, will be in market Fall 2025.

Find additional info at RenitaBryant.com or myndmatterspublishing.com.

Milton Keynes UK
Ingram Content Group UK Ltd
UKHW051410061024
449206UK00016B/115